TEMPEST IN THE WILDERNESS

FIREFIGHT AT SARATOGA . . . .

Rob clawed the sticky material from his face, suddenly realizing it was gelatinous, human tissue, the brains of a young Hessian's shattered head that had taken a direct hit by a cannon ball. Glancing at the decapitated remains nearby, his gut wrenched with nausea. Ian's dire warnings of horrific confusion in battle welled up in his mind. Why hadn't he listened more closely? He now knew that Father Henri's dire descriptions of hottest Hell paled in comparison to the ferocious roar and stench of todays pitched encounter.

But this fight wasn't supposed to be. Burgoyne himself had said that these rebels would run as they did at Hubbardton and were no match for the Royal Army. Head reeling, Rob peered helplessly over the breastwork to see a horseman driving hard upon his shelter.

Caleb raised his pistol to fire, but was too late as the horse and rider leaped among the Tories, the officer slashing away with his sword.

His senses finally kicking in, Rob recognized Benedict Arnold yelling to the on-rushing, wild-eyed rebels, "Boys, this way. Attack, Attack!" Caleb rose up, pistol in hand, but too late, Arnold's sword began its downstroke.

At nearly the same time, Tory musket balls slammed into both horse and rider, bringing them both down. Arnold tried to roll free, but his maimed leg was pinned beneath the thrashing, wounded horse.

TEMPEST IN THE WILDERNESS

A Novel about the American Revolution
On the Northern Frontier

Best wishes, Phyllis,
and good luck!

Win Lavallee

Winston Lavallee

To order additional copies of this book, contact:
Xlibris Corporation
1-888-795-4274
www.Xlibris.com
Orders@Xlibris.com
76387

Also by Win Lavallee

Dancing in the Dark
A Novel about the Civilian Conservation Corps

Short Stories

Why Rosa Won't Sing
Gynandromorph
Come Back to Sorrento
The Patriot
Medic
Screwdriver

For Peggins
And
Our children
Katherine, Christopher, Andrew, and Thomas
And Their Children

"Tis the gift to be simple,
tis the gift to be free,
tis the gift to come down
where we ought to be."

From an Old Shaker Hymn
By Joseph Bracket, Jr.
Alfred, Maine, 1848

"To be really free, one must live simply.
In war, the simple life flies away.
Mark me, no one becomes free
trying to destroy the other."

Ian MacKensie

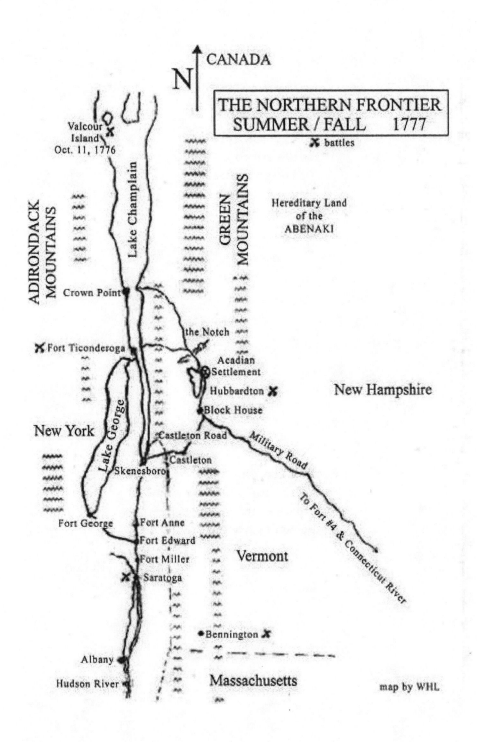

CANADA

N

THE NORTHERN FRONTIER
SUMMER / FALL   1777

✗ battles

Valcour
Island
Oct. 11, 1776

Lake Champlain

GREEN MOUNTAINS

Hereditary Land
of the
ABENAKI

ADIRONDACK MOUNTAINS

Crown Point

the Notch

Fort Ticonderoga

Acadian
Settlement

Hubbardton ✗

New Hampshire

Block House

Lake George

New York

Castleton Road

Castleton

Skenesboro

Military Road

Fort George

Fort Anne

Fort Edward

Fort Miller

Vermont

To Fort #4 & Connecticut River

✗ Saratoga

Bennington ✗

Albany

Hudson River

Massachusetts

map by WHL

PROLOGUE

THE LAKES

The land between present day Quebec, Canada and the Hudson River of New York is bounded on the west by the Adirondack Mountains of New York and on the east by the Green Mountains of Vermont. It is a pleasant, pastoral land despite its reputation for harsh, unfriendly winters and capricious summer storms. In this geological trough lie two important freshwater bodies, Lakes Champlain and George. Some think that in very ancient times these serpentine-shaped waters were a part of the huge Great Lakes system which lies many miles to the west. Indeed, the presence of New York's Finger Lakes and the scores of smaller lakes and ponds along the Champlain and George periphery would suggest that this is so. They are probably the melted and partially drained remnants of the last continental glacier that covered the area more than 15,000 years ago.

The lakes have a nearly uninterrupted 120-mile main axis, north/south, which made them a natural travel corridor for Native Americans and, after the 16th century when the Europeans arrived, for the movement of traders, settlers and supplies. During struggles between the English and the French for New World domination, these waterways became a hotbed of contention and bloody battles. After the French and many of their Abenaki Indian allies were defeated in 1761, colonists, mostly British, gradually settled the area near the lakes. But with the rebellion of the American colonies in 1775, war again roiled this bucolic land. The lakes as well as forts and the roads to and from them again became part of renewed military objectives.

The Iroquois had, long ago, aptly named the lakes, 'the door to the country". Guarding this door or merely passing through it was to be a dangerous venture full of surprises and dark and bloody business.

THE ABENAKI

The Abenaki were only one of the many eastern woodland native American tribes extending from present day New Brunswick, Quebec and Nova Scotia to Lake Champlain. Their northern boundary was roughly the St. Lawrence River and they could be found in parts of Maine, New Hampshire and Vermont as well as in river valleys to the south. These were the Abenaki hereditary lands. Distinct, but with much in common with surrounding tribes, they had lived in this region for thousands of years coping with sporadic tribal wars and extended periods of peace and trade with their neighbors, the Iroquois, the Penobscots and southern New England tribes.

Early on they had confronted French explorers sailing down the St. Lawrence. But the French, interested mainly in beaver pelts and baptisms, were not a serious threat to Abenaki culture and freedom. Indeed, many became converts to French Catholicism through the efforts of the "black robes", Jesuit missionaries sent by French kings. The French also intermarried with Abenakis and developed family ties among them as well as a special metis culture, which bridged the two groups. Despite accounts of savagery among and by the Abenaki, including the capture of white children and women, records exist of humane actions and a moral code superior to that of many Europeans.

Contact with Dutch fur traders in the Hudson Valley exacerbated the lucrative beaver pelt trade and slowly shifted tribal economies and culture toward European traditions. But population pressure from the south by the English colonists created friction from the mid-1600s on. After neutralizing the southern New England coastal tribes through war and disease, the English spread north and west seeking more territory for their food crops and animal fodder.

By the late 1600s, rival England and France became locked in recurring wars, which soon spread to their North American colonies. The Abenaki, noting the decline of the fur trade, mostly allied with the French and vigorously resisted English pressure on their lands. Repeated confrontations bred strong hatreds and resulted in vicious raids by both groups. In English homes, the name Abenaki became synonymous with the devil. After the surprise raid, destruction and massacre at the Abenaki town of Saint Francis, Canada in 1759 by Roger's Rangers, an elite colonial militia, the power and the spirit of these native folks was never the same.

1

GRANDE PRE 1755

Jean Hebert's ears had perked up at the first sounds of musketry in the village. He laid two recently slain ducks in the bottom of his bateaux and, looking over the water, observed smoke somewhere behind the high dune blocking his view of Grande Pre. He beached his craft and scrambled up the sand hill for a better view. Something was very wrong. He knew that British ships had dropped anchor off shore several days before. The men of Grande Pre had been invited to confer with Colonel Winslow, the British commander, and with representatives of Massachusetts Bay Colony regarding the loyalty of the Acadian folk.

The French Acadian settlers had for generations been pawns in French and English wars for control of North America. Both had demanded unquestioned loyalty to their respective sovereigns, but the settlers had wisely refuse to ally with either and sought to remain neutral. Largely ignoring the wars and diplomatic plots around them, the Acadians became efficient and prosperous farmers of their neatly sculpted bayside lands, a development not overlooked by greedy colonists to the south, many of whom wished to annex these lands as a 14th colony.

The Acadians had also developed close ties and harmonious trade with the original Native Americans, some intermarrying and generating a substantial metis population. It was a metis kinsman that Jean now saw running up the other side of the dune, dragging a young woman, Jean's wife, and her small child. Spying Jean on the crest, the metis cried out, "Non, non. Retourer!" Jean gathered them together and demanded an explanation. "The British. The British. They are removing families to the boats and destroying our houses and lands", his wife wailed, hugging the wide-eyed child. With the help of the metis they had escaped the redcoat round up of villagers.

Hebert locked hands around his musket and threatened to return to Grande Pre, but his wife pleaded with him. "They are separating families on different ships, some even parting children from parents. No one knows where they are going. We must stay together and scatter to the forest where our kinfolk, the Abenakis will care for us."

"What? And leave this land which our fathers have carefully tended?" he thundered.

"Oh, Jean, it is no longer ours. We are being deported."

Le Grande derangement had begun.

Finally convinced of his wife's argument, Jean urged them all into his bateaux. They would escape across the sometimes treacherous strait of Bay of Fundy water to the New Brunswick mainland where their metis kinsman knew they would find refuge. Fortunately, the September day was overcast and a thick fog was setting in, a not unusual event on the upper reaches of Fundy Bay. Muffling their oars, they eluded the British vessels and were soon swallowed up by the mist. Luckily the tide was not running high. Calling on strength built by years behind the plow, Jean's powerful arms soon propelled the bateau safely across the strait.

2

July 8, 1758
Fort Carillon
Lake George/Lake Champlain

Ian MacKenzie shouldered his musket and maintained his part of the thin red line. General James Abercromby had assigned the 42nd Regiment of Black Watch to be his point for the attack on Fort Carillon on the shores of Lake Champlain. Ian was in the New World only a month, having been a boy shepherd at the family's hard scrabble tenancy in the western highlands. The Scottish rebellion of Bonnie Prince Charlie had been crushed by the English at the slaughter of Cullendon only 12 years earlier. Pursuit and hangings of the defeated Scots had broken the highland clan system and left Ian's family destitute with but the marginal subsistence of a sheep tenancy. In a fit of desperation, his father had sold Ian into the British Army. Despite harsh military discipline and the separation, Ian had landed on his feet. Good food and the hard training had made him sinewy and tough as wire. His limited English prompted the training officers to assign him to the elite 42nd Scots commanded by the Campbells who had always been recognized as a tough lot. The Black Watch could be depended on to carry the field of battle.

But Ian wasn't feeling confident today. All the rumors predicted an easy win over the outnumbered French defending Fort Carillon. The colonials and regular British regiments were already toasting each other. Some said that the fort was incomplete and Brigadier Howe had found the weak spot in the walls. But why hadn't General Abercromby used his artillery? A few cannonballs over the ramparts might convince the French to give up without a fight and they could all return to camp. A minor skirmish a day ago had left Howe mortally wounded and the whispers rippling through the ranks didn't give much respect to Abercromby who, it was said, had used politics to rise to his position.

The first rank sergeant was giving "Present Arms", the preliminary to assuming firing positions. Still they marched forward, Major Campbell on a horse slightly to the rear, urging them on. Further to the rear, Abercromby and his staff were in discussion about the 42nd's thrust. He was being a bit indecisive, but his lieutenants were full of confidence and urged him to look at the disciplined ranks of the Black Watch. The closed ranks did appear invincible, even thrilling, as they moved toward the small copse shielding the rough earthworks of the French. These were nothing more than an abatis of tree trunks hastily thrown up near the unfinished vulnerable north wall of the fort. But as Ian and his rank moved closer, they could see a line of sharpened poles embedded among the tops of the felled trees. They would slow the attack, taking valuable time to remove for passage, all the while their being exposed to French musket fire. The lone bagpiper some twenty paces ahead of the front rank was skirling for the attack.

Finally, Abercromby was convinced. He rose in the stirrups and waved his sword forward towards the abatis. The Campbells cheered and gave orders to continue the march. The bagpiper moved away to the end of the rank, still playing, but getting out of the way of the 42nd's muskets. Ian was only 50 feet from the abatis when the order to halt and assume the firing position was given. In perfect unison, the front rank shouldered muskets and waited for the sergeant's order to fire. Suddenly, the felled trees spit flame and smoke. The waiting French had been patient, but were not about to let the Redcoats get the jump on them. Ian saw a number of men fall, but squeezed his trigger on the sergeant's command

A wall of smoke now separated the combatants. Ian's rank went immediately to a kneeling position and began to reload while the second rank shouldered weapons. Another volley of musket balls slammed into the abatis. Ian stayed low knowing that the third rank would fire over the heads of ranks one and two. His weapon was reloaded and upon the third rank's volley, he would rise and make his second shot. But he could see nothing, not even the spears of the defenders. He looked around, noting that many men had fallen. Some moved painfully, crawling towards the rear; others were ominously still. Several officers' horses were riderless and running uncontrolled into the ranks. The sergeants were trying to rally the survivors and close the ranks for another volley and a rush at the French position. But barely had the new volley been released, when there came another blast from the copse. Ian had not seen one Frenchman yet, but knew they had the upper hand. The sergeants screamed "Bayonets!" but the knotted Redcoats could barely free themselves from their wounded comrades. A few men, bayonets fixed and yelling wildly ran into the copse never to be seen alive again. Ian suddenly felt as if someone had struck him with a huge cudgel and when he tried to rise there was a strange numbness in his thigh causing him to tumble over the man next to him. He then saw that his leg was bent awkwardly just below the knee and blood was soaking his trousers. He joined others attempting to crawl to the rear, but went only several yards before passing out. His last sensation was that of bloody weeds entering his mouth.

He woke to a silence broken by moans of the wounded. Dead men lay around him and he searched the field for comrades who would soon come to gather the fallen. But the only ones walking on the field were the French who seemed stunned by the slaughter. They had pushed the Redcoats back beyond the stream that separated the two lakes and were now returning to the safety of their fort. Among them were Indians who looked for scalps to hang on their wigwams. They even attempted to scalp the living, but were stopped by the French commander. One Indian had scalped the bagpiper and, fascinated by the instrument, had run off into the copse with it, blowing insane sounds and moans. Ian lay still, not wanting to attract any attention. As the French started to leave the field, several Indians moved furtively out of the brush waiting for the opportunity for fresh scalps. One came onto Ian, who rolled over and attempted to grab the dirk sheathed in his anklet. But he lacked the strength to resist and saw the knife in the Indian's hand. After a single slice had been made, an explosion rang out and the Indian crumpled, adding his blood to that dripping from Ian's forehead. A badly wounded Black Watch officer some two yards away smiled through pale lips. In his hand was a smoking horse pistol. Ian tried to lift a hand in gratitude, but dropped into the darkness once more.

As the sun dropped lower in the west, the killing field became suddenly quiet, save for the moans of the few living survivors. The Scots would return for their own, but not until the protection of night. Now, several rough-clad farmers moved cautiously out of the woods, looking for booty and searching for weapons they could use for hunting. Upon reaching Ian, one muttered "Sacre bleu!" and called the other over. "He is alive! But unless he gets help he won't last the hour."

They wrapped the leg and head to slow the blood flow, then dragged him off the field. In the cover of the woods, the larger man hoisted him onto his shoulders while his partner shouldered the muskets and booty that included the horse pistol. They went deeper into the forest away from the fort and the British encampment, crossed the lake narrows and followed a path over boulder-strewn hills to a small subsistence farmstead and clearing. A woman ran to meet them and knew immediately what to do. After washing the wounds, she wrapped them in herbs and poultices, then had the men cut wooden splints to lash on the leg. They laid him on straw in the cowshed and instructed a young girl to sit with him by candlelight through the night. The woman returned at midnight and examined her handiwork. Ian moaned and asked for water that was immediately given. The woman smiled. "He will live."

Ian improved, but very slowly. A raging fever required the constant attention of the women so they moved him into their rough cabin. In a bizarre world, he understood nothing of their chatter and concern, nor could they discern his ravings. He must surely be dead and in another world. But he was grateful for the cool swabs on his face and body when the repeated crises had passed. After two weeks, he was able to keep down more than fluids and responded to the ministrations of the women and their presence. That they were French, he knew, but only by sign language could they communicate. And where was he? What had happened to the 42nd? The leg took longer to mend and wasn't a sight for the squeamish. The bones had knitted, but the knee would never be fully flexible. The women forced him to do domestic chores and to take care of himself, more for his own conditioning than from necessity. The men came and went, eyeing him with curiosity and amusement. One day, the elder woman's husband brought in a hand-drawn map and with a work-gnarled finger showed Ian where he was. The British had withdrawn to Fort Edward, leaving the French in control of the lakes.

They all realized that the young Scot was going to stay for a while and generously made a place for him conditioned on his making fair contribution to the family. These French were different from the enemy he recently confronted. They were too occupied wresting a living from the harsh New England soil to take sides in the larger war of the superpowers. He learned in time that they were Acadians who had been removed from their settlements by the English some years before and, with Abenaki help, had migrated into French Canada, then followed the Lake of Champlain south to this land beside the lake waters. Back in Acadia, water had always been their expertise and friend. They had developed fertile farmland from the Bay of Fundy salt marshes by means of a working system of dikes and flushing channels to hold back toxic ocean waters and to purge the saline soil with fresh water. Ian wondered how they could survive here among the Indian savages, but soon learned that many French had taken Indian wives and traded in peace with the natives.

While gratefully aware that his life had been saved by these folk, he yearned to rejoin his regiment, the only life he understood. As summer turned into fall, his everyday work with the family forced him to pick up enough French to communicate and to admire their industry as they prepared for winter. He would always have a bad limp and, when a month after the conflict, the elder woman held a looking glass before him, he winced at his appearance. The Indian's knife had left a long red scar that creased his forehead, giving him a permanent frown sure to scare young children.

As fall settled on the farm, Ian gave yeoman service to the family and took a regular place at their spare, but nourishing table. The half dozen other French families in the area shared labor in putting up forage and food for the winter and were impressed by this former enemy. His knowledge as shepherd made him a natural to care for the livestock and by the time winter locked in, he was given full responsibility for the animals some of which were sold to provision the defenders of Fort Carillon. Despite the wounds, Ian was a handsome lad and attracted the attention of a neighbor's daughter. By spring, he knew that his soldiering days were over and that he would make a family beside these waters. The subsistence farms lay close to a smaller lake that in ancient times had likely been an arm of Champlain. Enhanced by skilled farming practice, its shore provided nutritious grass and fodder for animals. The Acadians had cleared the forest back to provide even more animal space and used the wood for their abodes and outbuildings. Fish from its depths gave a rich diet, summer and winter. And it softened the rough appearance of the crude farm, framing the settlement in a most pleasant aura. In evenings, after chores, Ian and the young woman became frequent strollers along its shore.

Spring 1759 also brought warnings that another British force would try to take Fort Carillon. Abercromby was gone in disgrace, replaced by Sir Jeffery Amherst who had a reputation of winning battles and making decisions, not all of them benign, friend or foe, for those who resisted his will. The Acadians were uneasy, having been the pawns of the English before. When Amherst found that they had been feeding the defenders of the fort, he would exact more than their loyalty. The first winds of impending battle came with the visit of a small contingent of colonial rangers who had been sent to reconnoiter Fort Carillon. The women had come running from the field where spring planting had begun. Ian and the Frenchman met them near the cow stable where they were eyeing the livestock. Ian did most of the talking with the strangers who were rather taken aback at his presence and appearance. Their leader correctly noted that he must be a survivor of the previous summer debacle. After they left, the Frenchman's wife drew Ian aside and warned him of their likely return to press Ian back into the British ranks. He scoffed at this and swore he would not return to that killing field, especially now that his common-law wife's belly was swelling.

Amherst's campaign was a complete reverse of Abercromby's. Fort Carillon surrendered without a clash, the defenders having reduced it to a shell and retired north to Canada. The British presence was merely a new customer for food and fodder of the Acadians and they prospered. The British soldiers despite their knowledge of his location never sought Ian. They most likely concluded that a maimed soldier was more liability than asset.

3

Diary Entry: July 25, 1759
The Military Road

"Having recently taken Forts Carillon and Saint Frederic on Lake Champlain from the French, I now desire that a military road be established from our new fortifications at Crown Point to Fort #4 on the Connecticut River. This avenue through the mountain wilderness will permit rapid movement of troops and provisions to these defenses and secure forever the colonial northern frontier from depredations by the marauding French and their Indian savages. To this end, I have ordered its construction and have commissioned Captain John Stark of the New Hampshire militia and 200 yeomen of axe to commence work."

In His Majesty's Service,
Sir Jeffrey Amherst
Major General

When Amherst initiated his military road, his planners sought Ian's language fluency and knowledge of the area. The road would traverse the edge of the Acadians' lake before plunging into the forests to make its way over the Green Mountains to the Connecticut River. Ian's first born, a son called Rob, would grow up seeing frequent passage of arms, men and goods on their way to Forts Ticonderoga (the old Fort Carillon) and Crown Point.

The social and political effects of this new military route would go far beyond what Amherst ever imagined. Settlers from New York and particularly New England poured north after the peace accords between the French and English were signed in 1763. Rough forest paths previously trod only by Abenakis and Mohawks became interlocking dusty byways traversed by farmers moving their livestock and grains, lumber and other goods to the lakes and thence to markets in Albany and Montreal. The first pioneers, of course, took the most promising lands that soon would be coveted by those following. In no time, conflict between men of the New Hampshire Province and New Yorkers became commonplace. Yet for all this expansion and confrontation, whole tracts of the Green Mountains remained wilderness populated by trappers and small clusters of rural folk through whose veins surged French, Anglo-Irish, and Metis blood. Many of these people, including Abenaki remnants, became caught in conflicts they knew little about and in which they had no desire to be involved.

4

THE ACADIAN SETTLEMENT 1770

Father Henri thrust his oar cautiously now as he approached the narrows. Ahead lay the mouth of Purgatory Creek, his destination. He and his companion had paddled their canoe more than 70 miles down the east side of Champlain without incident. Nearly three score years old, he looked much younger, having kept fit by his peregrinations among the scattered Abenaki and metis settlements bringing them the sacraments and the Word of God. Priests were in short supply and after Montcalm and Quebec fell in 1759 few had continued to go among the settlements in the conquered lands of Vermont where the English-speakers held papists to be little better than the savages. The true believers he now sought hadn't seen a black robe in three years. How many baptisms, how many confessions, how many sins to forgive, how many unions to belatedly bless? These needs hung heavy on his mind. In truth, he knew that his scattered flocks had drifted away from old Catholic dogma. To survive in the wilderness required adaptations, body and soul. Their discard of the chaff of the mother church concerned him not so long as they still held to beliefs of love and forgiveness in the name of Jesus.

The person in the bow of the canoe, an Abenaki, had been his companion for more than a decade. She was something more than a helpmate, a relationship he refused to admit to his bishop, who, comfortably ensconced in Montreal, knew little of how his frontier priests lived. Someday he would have an accounting before Almighty God relying then on his Maker's profound forgiveness and, perhaps, a healthy sense of humor. Father Henri's failings were neither greater nor less than the souls to which he ministered.

No Hair was a survivor of the white man's plague that had taken so many of her tribe. Stricken just prior to the Ranger raid on St. Francis, she had escaped the massacre by remaining in the tiny isolated hut of the sachem who was trying to cure her. A bearded Ranger smashed his way in, slew and scalped the sachem, but left her, perhaps frightened by the fevered eyes and pustules covering her body. She was too weak to move, but experienced the psychological trauma of the scalping and the shrieks of relatives burning in their homes put to the torch by the looting Rangers. Father Henri had found her days later and carried her to the remains of the church where he prayed for her and soothed her disfigured body. In time she recovered, but the fever had caused the permanent loss of all her hair, hence the name given her by the returning Abenakis. Tribal members were astounded to find her, at least in their minds, risen from the dead. But most thought that the spirit of the dead sachem was within her. This caused trepidation and they would not tolerate her presence in the village. Father Henri did his best to tell them that her recovery was God's will, but her bald head and pockmarked face was a ghostly and frightening reminder of their loss.

Father Henri fashioned her a protective cap and took her to his settlement so she might gain strength. But even there, the French and metis barely accepted her. Despite church propriety, he kept her in his own lodgings and in time assisted in his rounds serving his flock. A quick study, she soon acquired knowledge and understanding befitting a sachem. And her adulation of Father Henri knew no bounds. Only he could calm her infrequent fits of monstrous panic disorder when she recalled the massacre.

Down lake and across the narrows loomed Crown Point. In years past both this fort and Carillon some miles beyond had welcomed him and other French entourages. That was long ago. The British and colonials there now would warn him away. Black robes might come and go to visit their flocks, as there was no wish to rile the resident French. The danger came from rogue bands of English and Mohawks who made sport and money from scalps of the unwary. Black robe scalps, still at a premium, caused him to shed the cassock and don frontier garb. Only the white collar and an inscribed cross remained hidden beneath his rustic overshirt. They slid silently into the sluggish, broad creek waters as inconspicuous trappers.

Four miles upstream they beached the craft and hid it beneath a tangled blowdown. The final distance to the Acadian settlement would be on foot. No Hair, armed only with a French pistol hidden in her sash, led the way. She had an unerring sense of direction and extremely keen ears. Father Henri followed some twenty paces behind. He had a knife sheathed by his waist, more for authentic appearances than protection. His Christian values would never permit him to kill another human. Several miles from the creek, No Hair hesitated. Somewhere ahead were human voices. Father Henri knew that they were close to the military road leading to Crown Point and surmised that these were part of the garrison.

"Let them pass", he silently signaled to No Hair.

After a half-hour wait, they continued, soon emerging from the brush onto the military road that would lead them to the Acadians. As they were rounding a bend where a cut in the Green Mountains narrowed the road, No Hair again signaled caution. Too late. Emerging from hiding behind jagged rocks strewn there by glacier eons before, three Mohawks and a white man blocked their way.

Father Henri rose to the challenge by hailing them as fellow travelers. They would have none of this and demanded valuables. The priest handed them a small purse containing a few shillings prepared for just such an event. In the transfer, the hidden cross inadvertently slid into sight. The Mohawks stepped back in sudden fear of the symbol, but the white man grinned malevolently and demanded it. No Hair, largely ignored up to now, edged out of the circle, opened her tunic and raised the pistol. With lightning speed, the Mohawks reacted, but not before the weapon fired and dropped the closest one in his tracks. The others hesitated, but Father Henri's knife was out and trembling in his hand, very close to the white man's throat. "Partir encourant, No Hair. Partir encourant!" he thundered, before becoming backed up against the rocks. She flew and disappeared into the brush as he lowered the knife. To give more assurance of her escape, he again raised the knife and, crying out, "Forgive me, Jesus", threatened a slash at the white man's throat. The brigand easily sidestepped the weapon that then plunged deep into an approaching savage. The Mohawk groaned and grasped the knife and his split gut, falling backwards onto his dying kinsman. The white man, quickly recovering from the priest's unexpected attack, deftly thrust his own knife into Father Henri's heart.

When it was over, the two remaining marauders stripped Father Henri's body of the cross and other valuables. The Mohawk took the priest's scalp and hauled his colleagues' bodies into the brush to molder away, hidden from sight and discovery by only carnivorous scavengers. No Hair, fearing that she was followed, ran swiftly, realizing that safety for both her and her savior was the Acadian settlement. Exhausted, she fell into the arms of a woman working in the fields who alarmed Ian, his wife and the other men of the misfortune. They quickly found the carnage and mourned dreadfully over Father Henri's remains. The Acadians wanted to pursue the murderers, but Ian advised caution. With the harm already done, nothing would be gained. Amid wailing and sorrow, they buried the savages. Father Henri's body was carried to the settlement and interred in a plot near the lake. The disconsolate No Hair was taken in by the settlement. The Acadians overlooked her disfigurement, as they had Ian's, and she became a much-trusted counselor in Abenaki ways as well as beloved mentor to Rob.

5

May 24, 1774
Boston, Massachusetts Bay Colony

Joshua Shattuck roused himself from the palette he'd been given in the cramped little room under the eaves. For too long into the night he had spent reading the tattered volumes brought from England, gifts of the kindly Cornwall physician. There was little to love in this city, but books were his salvation and most of them he had committed to memory. It was nowhere near dawn, but he must get the charcoal lit in the downstairs forge. Since the previous spring, he'd been the Barton Brothers Ironmongers boy servant. He was not a strapping lad, often given to bouts of ague and fever, conditions not helped by the daily exposure to the fumes of the forge and the strains of lugging sheet iron into the shop for rendering. All the human ailments of 1774 Boston seemed to be taking their turn on him. Of late, he'd developed a persistent cough that sapped his limited strength. But summer was here at last and a fresh breeze blew into Boston harbor as he slipped down the narrow stairway to the shop.

The Barton brothers, Ethan and Noah, would not be up for an hour, but would expect their forge to be work ready. Not that they were very effective at the smithy early in the day, having spent the night before drowned in rum. That was what really frightened Joshua, having them at the forge with demon rum addling their brains. They were competent ironsmiths to be sure and the Boston market for their products had made them rich. But the two stingy bachelors shared nothing with others and could be most cruel, especially when under the influence.

Josh eyed their living quarters on the far side of the shop, its huge iron-clad door shut tight and secured, he knew, on the other side against intruders seeking to plunder them. He'd never ventured in there. As an indentured servant that was not his place as the Bartons had frequently reminded him. He suspected that they kept a small fortune hidden, but he coveted nothing of theirs. He just wanted to complete his indenture, get out of the fetid city and seek success in the west, maybe in the Connecticut colony. It was said that New Haven had a climate and ambience similar to Cornwall from whence he came. He nourished recollections of the time he had spent working with his father, a gardener, at the manor house in Cornwall with its lush gardens and park, the kindness of the local vicar who taught him to read and write his name and his early apprenticeship to the village physician. That had all been truncated when his father died suddenly and he and his mother had been turned out of the small cottage and forced to cope on the roads and countryside. She soon married again and it became clear that Josh was not to be part of the new family. So this indenture, a common practice of the day, was arranged.

"Ah well, no daydreams today," he sighed. "The forge awaits."

An hour later, in the small bloomery, Josh lit the charcoal to make it ready for iron ore which when brought to the required high temperature would "bloom" and release the raw iron ready for beating and folding by the brothers. But still nothing had stirred from the Barton quarters. He was getting hungry, expecting a brother to unlatch the door and slide a tray with some meager fare his way. At least it would fortify his day and sustain him. He eyed the door again, then came closer to listen. Nothing. Maybe they had never returned from the Queen's Purse that kept them well supplied with grog. Hesitating, he lifted a hand to rap, then grasped a small branding iron nearby, using it as a knocker. Silence from within. He pushed the door slightly and was astonished when it gave way easily. Glancing inside, he was repulsed by the squalor, but had expected nothing more. No one home. A sudden urge came over Joshua to leave this place, this city, and his indenture and make way to the west. Others had done it and were free. He would be sought after and if captured, knew that he faced an extended commitment. But the fresh summer wind now blowing through the shop entry was particularly enticing.

He mounted the tiny stairway to gather a small sack of belongings, then dashed back down and out the entrance, nearly knocking down one of the brothers who was staggering over the entry in a state of some intoxication. As Josh regained balance and kept going, the brother thundered after him, "You're not getting away, you scum. You owe me and Noah about five more years." Joshua continued running. Once he mingled with the rousing population, the Bartons would never find him, especially in their stupor. By nightfall, he would be on his way west. Too late he saw the leg stuck out to trip him. He tumbled to the cobblestones, bruising his hands and forehead. Dazed, he sat up and looked into the face of Noah, who, bleary-eyed, was being escorted home by loud and laughing drinking companions.

Noah, despite the dissipation of rum, was strong as a bull, made fit by the work at the forge, He bent Josh's arms behind him until they nearly cracked and hauled him back to the shop. His brother grinned malevolently and pointed to a chair in the corner. "What in hell do you think you're doing, slave boy?" Josh locked eyes with a furious glare. "Noah, open that there bottle and let's have a toast to the slave's next five, no, let's make it ten years here. That's what you get for running away and we got witnesses." Both brothers took a long drink, then another. They could hold great quantities of liquor. Ethan had the small branding iron in his hand. "When I come in, our door was open and this iron on the floor. You was never to go in there. How come, slave boy? Maybe you was about to rob us?" Josh glared, rubbed his arms and reflected on his stupidity, but knew he was never going to last another ten years at the forge. "Just couldn't find you after the fire was hot. And I needed some food." As if reading his mind, Noah returned to lock the sore arms behind him again, telling the brother to put the iron in the fire.

The brand was a device for marking leather products, a favorite tool of the tanner's trade. This one the Barton brothers had made to mark their own products and consisted of a small double B to signify Barton Brothers or BB. Josh immediate saw what Noah was up to and nearly broke the big man's grasp, but only got sharp pain in the badly angled arms. Flinging him face down on the shop floor, he had Ethan hand him the glowing iron. No matter how Josh twisted, he was held fast. Laughing as only uncontrollable drunks can, the brothers watched as the neck flesh behind both of Josh's ears simmered and smoked like a piece of bacon. The sickly sweet smell of roasted skin, his own, filled Josh's nostrils as he screamed in agony. It was over in seconds, but the pain was nearly unbearable. Bloody fluid oozed down his neck. The brothers watched him without pity. "You'll be all right, slave boy. That's just a lesson to you not to run. Won't have no trouble finding you now with that double B." They roared with insane laughter. "You're a Barton Bastard now!"

Josh dashed to the fire bucket of cold water and immersed his head to stanch the burn. The brand had grazed the surface muscles of his neck, but they still worked. The pain was incredible and he knew there would be permanent scarring. Ethan and Noah recovered from their glee and told him to get his apron on and commence the day's work, never offering any breakfast. He did as he was told despite the grievous wounds and trauma which left him shocked and light-headed. He'd get through this, but his next try for freedom would be a success even if his life depended on it.

6

October 2, 1774

"Bring that there kettle to the forge and dump those jugs of molasses in. C'mon, let's be quick about it!"

Josh did as he was told, all the while curious about this strange order. He'd heard the commotion down the street from the shop, but was never allowed to leave the forge unattended, even to steal a look from the doorway to the shop. Both he and the Bartons were well aware of the danger of a blaze among the hovels of Boston.

Soon the molasses was beginning to steam a bit and had become runny and slick. Noah put his finger in, then jerked it out and sucked the wet heat before it burned him, remarking, "That'll do it". Coming through the door with a large sac over his shoulder was one of the drinking cronies, a giant called Justice. Justice often spent time at the shop, regaling the brothers, relating his amorous conquests and expressing his anger about the British soldiers patrolling the waterfront. He was a cunning culprit who always managed to side-step danger and blame. Josh was more frightened of him than the Bartons, reading a simmering cruelty and meanness in his eyes.

"Get outta the way, Dogshit." Justice shoved Josh aside and told the brothers to get a move on.

They left the shop with their burdens and joined the mob gathering strength down the street. Josh checked the forge, then strained a look at the mob from the doorway. It wasn't pretty. The low-life of Boston had cornered a customs officer of the Crown and had him backed against a pier piling, yelling all sorts of epithets. As the abuse grew, any dignity the man had evaporated and he bolted in Josh's direction. The mob descended and commenced to rip off the poor man's cloak and badge of rank. From the horde, Justice and the Bartons appeared and Josh finally got the drift. It was to be humiliation with tar and feathers. After the man was stripped near naked, Noah dumped the hot molasses over him, despite his shrieks and screams, followed by Justice's loosing his sac of chicken and goose feathers. Although burning with pain, the now grotesque creature ran right by Josh, only to slip and roll on the cobblestones. The mob was beside itself with laughter and from somewhere a wheelbarrow appeared. The abused official was unceremoniously dumped in and the raucous mob formed a mock honor guard on each side of the barrow.

Josh was appalled by the cruelty, but dared not thwart the mob and found himself cheering along with them, yet retreating beneath the safety of the shop lintel. Suddenly the hubbub died as a patrol of Redcoats swung around the corner. Momentarily stunned by the scene, they gave the mob time to dissipate into the alleys and rat holes of the waterfront. There was no sign of Justice or the Bartons as the soldiers gingerly removed the whimpering customs man from his carriage and half-carried him to the nearest horse trough where his sticky coat was washed away revealing red splotches of burned skin. He was then led away to their military surgeon who would treat his injuries.

An hour later, the brothers and Justice slunk into the shop, chuckling wickedly. Josh busied himself at the forge and wouldn't look at them. They broke open a bottle and toasted their adventure.

"What's a matter, Dogshit?" yelled Justice between swigs. "You think you're better than us?"

Josh ignored the challenge and kept pumping the forge until a hand grasped his shoulder and spun him nearly to the floor. "You remember this, boy! You was part of the party out there awhile back. We saw you cheering us on. And don't forget who heated up the molasses when some soldier comes poking around to find us. Tell 'em anything and you'll get whipped as hard as us and when they is done, you'll get more stripes from us, right boys?" He was joined in laughter from the Bartons. Josh simmered inside and would not let it show, but he was now doubly sure that his remaining days in Boston were going to be few.

7

April 19, 1775

The entire city was on edge. The Redcoats had been forming up and drilling daily to impress the restless citizens. General Thomas Gage, Commandant of His Majesty's troops in Boston chafed at the open resentment of the colonials toward his splendid army. He knew who some of the troublemakers were, but stubbornly relied on his persuasive powers and a reasonable sense of justice to calm the waters. He always had the force of arms as backup if they were needed. Most alarming were reports of arms and gunpowder being stored in surrounding towns where the army could not easily find them. Each time he sent out the troops to grab this contraband, whispers of his plans leaked out. He soon would make another raid on the colonial powder magazines. But this time not even his closest staff officers would get prior plans. Orders would come from Gage alone on the morning of the event.

Josh rose just like he had done hundreds of times. He lit the forge. The coarse, rum-induced snoring of his masters on the other side of the ironclad door verified their condition and location. What they didn't know was that today he would make his escape. He'd carefully planned it to include a bogus ad for employment from a New Haven firm that he would leave carelessly under his palette. The brothers would find it and, illiterate themselves, have it read to them by their friends at the Queen's Purse.

While they searched in New Haven, he would be on his way elsewhere and in time become absorbed somewhere on the frontier. The Bartons had kept a sharp eye on him since his last dash, but he had squirreled away both money and food to get him on his way. He would survive by hiring himself out to farmers on a short-time basis until he was sure he was beyond the clutches of the brothers.

He gathered his stores and a few treasured books, then casually slipped out the door, making sure it was secure behind him. It was too easy, he thought, as he walked away from the waterfront. Few were stirring at this time, but shop doors were swinging open and farmer's carts were arriving at the open market. Where were the Redcoats?

Usually, the night watch was changing at this hour and the clank of military equipment could be heard. Josh slowed and eyed an ox cart that had unloaded and was turning around to go back over Boston Neck, a scrawny patch of dry land flanked by tidal marshes and bearing the single conduit to the mainland. Surely there would be guards near the 24 pounders aimed down Roxbury Road, defending the Neck. Usually Redcoats didn't bother young lads entering or leaving Boston, but this morning Josh wanted no questions. He fell in behind the cart and made like he was part of the delivery. The driver up front never noticed and as they approached the checkpoint, Josh hoisted himself aboard the cart. The soldiers waved them through rather hurriedly which pleased the farmer who gently goaded his beasts and continued towards Roxbury. As they rounded a bend, out of sight of the Redcoats, the farmer halted and leapt down to stand in front of his passenger, giving him the once over.

"Where you going, boy?"

"Visiting my brother's family in Concord." Josh lied.

The farmer's hard stare softened a bit. "Not the time to go. Them lobsterbacks at the Neck will be mighty suspicious with all the anger in Boston and the towns hereabouts." He bent closer as if someone might be overhearing them. "Word's out that old Gates has them on the march right now heading for Concord. There's going to be a scuffle, mark my words! Your brother may be waiting for them now at the bridge."

Josh hunched his shoulders, not so much in indifference as to hide the Barton tattoos on his neck. Of all the luck, to be in the middle of a fight. He'd soon be missed and the Barton brothers would be right on his tail if he stopped now. But he forced a grin.

"Looks like I'd better be on my way to help the family at the farm if he's trying to push the Redcoats back into Boston." He thanked the farmer for the ride and continued up the Concord Road.

"Well, don't say I didn't tell ya!" yelled the farmer who had turned off towards Roxbury.

Josh made the ten miles to Lexington in good time, noticing the increasing number of farmers, old and young, slogging along with him. Most were armed with muskets and other rather ominous looking weapons which normally cut and gathered crops. He felt secure among them, as the Bartons would have trouble locating him in this crowd. At Lexington Green he turned north and kept going, leaving his fellow travelers to greet the English. Now the colonials, some rather wild-eyed, were going in the reverse direction as he waved them on and let knots of them pass. By nightfall he had reached Bedford. All hell was breaking loose behind him as Gates' foray into Concord had stirred up a hornet's nest of angry minutemen. He was tired and hungry, but sought out an isolated sheep shed not far from the thoroughfare, ate his meager supply of food and was soon snoring lightly among the lambs on the pungent straw.

He was up before light and on his way, putting as much space between himself and Boston as he could muster. Two days later he was in the New Hampshire Province on the road to Fort Stephen, old Fort Number 4. Farms were scattered now and he felt safe enough to offer his labor for a day or so in return for meals and lodging. His upbringing on the Cornwall estate had given him skills that he now put to good use. Farmers asked him what the hell was going on down in Concord, but he feigned ignorance, saying he hailed from Rhode Island and didn't know much about that except for rumors that General Gates was pretty sore. After a day or two he would move on, always keeping to the road towards the frontier.

Two weeks later he was at Fort Number 4 on the Connecticut River. His ear always to the ground, he heard all the buzz in the garrison about the Concord battle that by now had traveled far and wide in the colonies. Rumors flew that Fort Ticonderoga had fallen to a small band of Green Mountain farmers. But all of this washed over Josh who revealed little about himself other than he needed work. It took a week's labor at the fort in barter for flint and steel, an ancient, but serviceable fowling piece, ball and powder and another day with a pioneer farmer to replenish his food supply. Thinking that he may have stayed too long at the fort, he soon scrambled onto the river ferry. But his confidence grew when in fine June weather he began trudging up the military road which would take him over the Green Mountains. This was unsettled country now with little opportunity to hire out or find shelter. He knew that the easier choice was to stay next to the river, but his fears of detection made him chose the wilds. This rough-hewn track traversing more than 70 miles to the lakes in the northwest was his ticket to freedom.

He had learned from soldiers at Fort Number 4 that a number of blockhouses had been constructed at intervals to provide protection in the event of Native American depredations. But with the French withdrawal years earlier, these small forts were anachronisms as the Indians, decimated by disease, were scarce and most of the healthy had gradually migrated to Canada along with the French. The blockhouses varied in construction, depending on the builders and their supplies of raw materials. Spaced roughly a day's march apart, most of them on this frontier were made of massive 15 inch cut oak logs arranged log cabin style in a square, roughly 20 by 20 feet, and 30 feet high at the peak of its hip roof. Stairs led to a loft-like second story overhang with fire ports opening to all sides and below, allowing defense against attack from any quarter. Now abandoned except for infrequent use by small bands of soldiers, British and colonial, and with even less frequent use by settlers, they were but mute reminders of earlier conflict.

The blockhouse Josh came upon late on the second day after a tiring haul over rough country stood on a small rise. He had slept the previous night in rain-drenched woods and this appeared to be just the place to dry out and get some real sleep. He pushed open the continuous batten, heavy, ironclad door and went in. Soldiers who had used it recently had left it a pigsty with uneaten game remains and other debris strewn over the dirt floor. He threw out the half-consumed animal corpses and discarded clothing, then ate his dwindling food horde and lay in some straw on the loft, falling immediately into deep slumber. He woke several times in the night as a thunderstorm passed over the mountains. The straw seemed terribly sharp and itchy, but he was too exhausted not to drift back into sleep.

When he arose, it was late morning. Not much light penetrated the small fire ports to dispel the dank gloom inside the fort. He rolled over in the straw and noticed the row of welts on his arm. Tiny flecks of blood had oozed and hardened there and itched like hell. He'd seen the same on other lads in Boston and knew the signs of bedbugs. "Damn!", he cried aloud and scuttled to his feet only to see hordes of flat, reddish-hued insects making off with blood, his blood, and scurrying away into the straw and cracks in the loft. They must have been starved since their last meal as Josh discovered more than a score of penetrations on his arms and legs and knew many more were on his neck and back. Even his face was bloody as he noted when rubbing his cheeks. He also knew that if he could stand the intense itch and not swell, he wasn't in any danger from the bites. The Bartons had been living with them for years and he had avoided them only by being scrupulously clean in his tiny garret. It was time to get out of this place and back on the road.

He started to put his leg on the loft ladder only to learn that he wasn't the only occupant of the blockhouse. Directly below him was a man wrapped in skins and a tattered blanket. Startled at first, Josh would not dare descend until he got a firm grasp on his fowling piece.

The stranger was tall, lean and stank to high heaven. Josh tried to step over him and get to the door, but was immobilized by an iron grip on his ankle. He spun around and pressed the muzzle of his gun into the grimacing face of an Indian. The grip was released and the stranger fell back onto his rag bed. Only then did Josh see the old musket propped against the wall and the festering wound on the stranger's arm. Beads of sweat stood out on the face and the lips were curled in pain. Josh scrambled to the doorway and threw it open, flooding the interior with bright sunlight. The Indian scowled and turned away as Josh bolted outside, then hesitated. Keeping his gun leveled on the Indian, he told him to come out and stand next to the wall. To Josh's surprise, the stranger answered in broken, but discernable English.

"I'm very sick! Arm is swollen with evil spirits. Need help!"

Sensing a trick, Josh considered sprinting up the road to a safer place, but knew that would be folly as the stranger's musket might easily bring him down and he had left behind his cache of food and extra clothing. The Indian emerged slowly and leaned against the timbers beside the door. Sans the dirty blanket, he wore leather leggings and a mixture of colonial garb. He clutched the wounded arm that in the sunlight looked septic, indeed. The lean face bore numerous pox scars that Josh knew spelled trouble. Few of the Native Americans had survived the White Man's Pox and he feared that those remaining were carriers. With his weapon, Josh had the upper hand and by the looks of the stranger, he had little to worry about so long as he kept his distance.

"What do they call you"?

"I am Tomsoc, Leaping Deer, so named because I move quickly in the woods. A week ago I fell onto sharp boulders and last night in the storm came here for shelter. This arm is useless now, but you must find ferns and herbs to chase the spirits out".

Josh thought for a time, then put the gun away. "Just don't come near me as you may have the pox. I will do what I can to heal the arm."

Tomsoc smiled and bowed his head to show Josh he meant no harm.

Josh gathered ferns from the wet area near the brook and lichens from the north side of maples. In his garret at the end of day's work he had read of herbal medicines in the books brought from Cornwall. But other than self-treating his traumatic branding, he had never used what he learned and now had to rely on the stranger to assist him.

"Go to the clear area near the road where little green plants flourish and find spiny seeds and leaves of burdock. Also, take my knife and scrape the bark of sweet-smell fir for sap. Bring these and mix ferns and lichens with them in hot water. When cool, spread these herbs over and into my wound. Then gather oak leaves for wrapping. With their bitters the spirits will be gone"

Josh was startled by the size and sharpness of Tomsoc's knife and wondered how many scalps it had sliced off. The Indian smiled, reading Josh's fear, but merely handed the weapon over, handle first. Josh did as he was told, taking care not to touch any poxy skin. Returning with vegetation, he wrapped the arm and added more ferns, hickory and oak leaves and some of the cleaner rags strewn about the floor. Tomsoc never flinched during his care and afterwards lay down on a bed of white pine needles that Josh had mounded in a sunny spot near the fort's wall.

Keeping a safe distance, Josh learned that Tomsoc belonged to an eastern woodland tribe called the Abenaki. Even Boston had known of their depredations on the frontier, first fighting English colonial expansion on their own, then as mercenaries for the French. Nearly as fierce as the Mohawks, their raids, plunder and kidnapping of children for ransom and new tribal members made them pariahs of the settlers who for more than 100 years had been systematically pushing them off their ancestral lands and spreading their European diseases among them. They were largely agricultural folk living in small enclaves, yet retained a semi-nomadic style that coveted essential hunting territories. Counter-raids by the English had nearly broken this culture and the diseases had reduced their numbers by half. Tomsoc, himself, had originally been part of a praying Indian tribe and had gone to a white man's Indian school where he learned English. He had run away to the north when the preacher, to whom he was servant, set about undermining Indian culture and converting his charges to the ways of the English.

"The preacher named me Jeffrey," he spat out bitterly; "but I am Tomsoc." He thrust out his lower lip in defiance. He then related that his tribe had nearly died off from white man's disease. Rumor had it that years before, the English military commander, Sir Jeffrey Amherst, had distributed gifts of pox-laden blankets to the natives to hasten their demise. Tomsoc had survived the pox only through the intercession of the Great Spirit and then joined the Abenaki. After regaining his strength, he would continue on the road to the lakes where a few of his tribe remained.

Josh was not convinced that Tomsoc's tale was totally accurate, but he was already thinking ahead. If Tomsoc could be trusted, it would be better for the two of them to travel together, sharing support and food from the hunt. And that old musket deer killer against the wall was worth five fowling pieces. It meant remaining here another day or two until the wound started to heal, but with the ado in Boston, it was unlikely that the Bartons would follow soon. Tomsoc was a kindred spirit, as much a refugee as he was.

He grew uncomfortable as the Indian focused on his neck scars, but decided that he would tell of his indenture and experiences in Boston. Tomsoc listened silently and intensely, merely nodding as Josh finished. Then he turned on his bed of pine needles and soon was snoring in the sun. Very little was said for the next two days. Tomsoc's wound healed rapidly and by the third morning he felt strong enough to continue up the military road. No sooner were they under way than Tomsoc noted that others had been rapidly traversing this very road by horse some weeks before. They would soon learn that Gates had stirred up more than a Boston hornet's nest.

*   *   *

On an evening in early May 1775, two men glared at each other over a table in the smoky Castleton, Vermont village tavern. One was swarthy, handsome, educated, and ambitious, a Connecticut merchant, recently commissioned colonel by the Massachusetts Committee of Safety and sent on a mission to quickly secure Fort Ticonderoga. The other, a farmer, rough-hewn, tough as an ox, a self-appointed colonel of a rag-tag group known as the Green Mountain Boys who for years had been the bane of the Yorkers, Albany colonists who claimed the mountain land west of the Connecticut River. Neither could admit it, but each colonel depended on the other to pull off their plan. In two weeks they and their "army" of four score farmers from the Massachusetts Berkshires and Green Mountains would assault the prize fort on Lake Champlain. Trouble was, the merchant, Benedict Arnold, had no troops. The other, Ethan Allen, needed whatever authority Arnold might have as a representative of the Massachusetts Committee. Arnold may have been a glory-seeker, but was also a realist and soon agreed to be joint commander with Allen, knowing full well that the Green Mountain Boys would answer only to Allen. On May 10, a befuddled garrison of English soldiers fell to these colonial raiders, who secured control of the lake corridor and much needed cannon for the fledgling Continental Army forming up outside of Boston.

*   *   *

Josh and Tomsoc crested the last hill of the western Green Mountains and took in the vast panorama of the Champlain Valley and the lakes. Farther to the west, in the distance, rose the Adirondacks. Tomsoc smiled and told Josh that his people were near and by late afternoon they could see smoke rising from several farms near the edge of sparkling waters. They entered the small, scattered compound of subsistence farms at suppertime and, to Josh's surprise, after some curious looks and careful questions, were welcomed as family.

The families greeting them were of metis stock, a mixture of French and Native American. But among them was a light-skinned man with a limp and savagely scarred face who looked upon Tomsoc's arrival with less than enthusiasm. But this season meant preparations for harvesting summer crops and every new set of hands was needed. Tomsoc could stay if he contributed to the efforts. Josh wasn't so sure even as he appreciated the largess of these farming folk. He was duly impressed with the skill and tidiness by which the people lived. Their fields and flocks were tended as scrupulously as any he had seen in Cornwall. A new orchard of fledgling apple trees caught his attention. But he could barely understand their talk save that of the limp and his son, Rob, a boy of Josh's age. Fortunately, his bonding with Rob was immediate and despite differences in dialect and disposition, observers would soon think of them as brothers.

Rob MacKensie was Ian's only child, a second son having been stillborn. His father's cultural difference played but a small role as he was woven into the Acadian fabric. Ian was terrifically proud of his boy, but could reflect a Scot's dour and taciturn disposition. By contrast, Rob's mother was a loving soul with an extremely sensible and happy nature who made sure that Rob deeply abided in the extended Acadian family. He learned Acadian ways, ate Acadian food and did his full measure of work in the settlement. Taller and lighter complexioned, he stood out from his relatives, but in all other ways was one of them. No Hair, the adopted Abenaki, had made sure that he understood her heritage and vital forest skills and, when Rob's mother died of fever in the winter of 1772, became a mother surrogate.

Few of the French-Canadians could read or write even rudimentary French. Father Henri had tried to encourage these skills, but his visits had been few and far between with precious little follow-up. It was up to Ian, who had a limited command of English, to make sure that the growing number of American colonists did not take advantage of his kinfolk.

As Rob matured, he savored the camaraderie of his relatives. Parties and dances at the end of the harvest season and into the winter were joyous events for all and no one enjoyed them more than Rob. He was popular with the young women any one of whom was hoping, in time, to be more than his friend. Amalie, a distant cousin, grew especially close. She had many of the ways of Rob's mother, but cleverly kept any obvious similarities out of their relationship. Most everyone except Rob could see a match, soon to come to fruition.

Despite Josh's careful habit of wearing his hair long to mask the BB scars, Ian had spotted the brand almost immediately and frowned in wonder at just how it got there. Josh related his recent past to Rob and Ian, both of whom flinched visibly from the tale. Both instantly promised keep the story within the settlement and to ignore any further inquiries about the double B.

The fall of Fort Ti to Ethan Allen's Green Mountain boys was about to change the lives of these rural folks forever. These same events soon made up Josh's mind. He would stay. Small groups of armed farmers passed through the settlement on their way home south, telling of the fort's fall as a great victory for the rebellion. With the British gone, more pioneers would soon be snapping up the lands of King George III. A week later several horsemen came beating down the road from the big lake, looking for a night's lodging. Astute and no slouches when it came to business opportunities, the Acadians had provided a roof for the occasional paying guest for years and, under Ian MacKensie's urging, had begun building a rustic inn for travelers.

Ian MacKensie viewed the handsome, swarthy officer and his two aides with the same disdain he had for Josh and Tomsoc, but the legal tender in Benedict Arnold's hand was too good to pass up. At supper that evening the guests retold of the fall of the fort which they said would herald a bright future for the new nation forming in Boston and the colonies to the south. Both Josh and Rob were completely taken in by the guests' narrative, elan and smart military dress, a reaction not missed by Arnold who said little, but clearly was looking for strong young men to join him. Ian sat near the fire, smoking his pipe and frowning through all the happy talk. When one of the aides tried to get his reactions, he arose and left the room, mumbling "There'll be no press gangs welcome here."

When Josh learned of Arnold's imminent return to Boston, he quickly lost interest and glanced at Tomsoc who had remained silent in the shadows, barely visible in the guttering candlelight. Helping one of the aides to saddle up next morning, Josh and Rob were each given several shillings and a prediction. "Colonel Arnold will be chasing the British out of Boston soon, mark my words." They then mounted and were soon out of sight around a bend in the military road, heading for the Connecticut River.

Ian joined them as they watched their guests depart. "They be off to new adventures, boys, but not what they think. War becomes full of bad things and blood. Brother insults brother. Neighbor against neighbor. The simple life flies away. They talk freedom, but many snares will rule. Mark me, no one becomes free trying to destroy the other."

8

There were hundreds of tasks at the subsistence farm cluster to be completed and Ian saw the presence of these two new and willing workers as a Godsend. He promised them good wages plus food and shelter if they would stay. Now isolated from the winds of war, the Acadians fell to the routine tasks of successful farming. Except for the infrequent dispatch riders to and from Boston, nothing disturbed them. Josh finally had the camouflage and security he needed and the work, although arduous, was free from the smells of Boston and was what, in his Cornish heart, he knew best. He lent yeoman service to the vegetable and herb gardens, keeping the weeds and varmints at bay and showing the women how best to take advantage of the Vermont sun and to extend their food growing areas into the rich soil of the lake edge while avoiding the water-logged clays.

At Ian's behest, he had examined the new orchard of snow apples to find that in the previous winter rodents had severely girdled the thin-skinned saplings. Using his hands, Josh measured the damage as he had been taught by his father, then stepped back and announced, "Bridges. They need bridges."

Ian and his extended family looked perplexed for a time. But when Josh explained how to graft the damaged trees, the Acadians were impressed.

"It may be too late, but if some of the limb sprouts can be gathered as scions, we may save these." He examined the flower buds that continued to ooze their sugary spring sap preparatory to breaking.
"See? These tell that there is still time if we hurry."

Rob and Josh spent the better part of two days slashing out the old torn bark wounds and tapping in small tin hooks to hold the scion bridges in place. At Josh's direction, Ian came right behind using his knife to bevel the ends of the scions and then inserting them behind the hooks into slits cut by Josh in the wounds of the living tree tissue. Rob followed with a tub of softened wax which he smeared over the wound, making sure that no air got to the connections between the embedded scions and the freshly made slits. "Got to keep them from drying," cautioned Josh.

Rob took on the appearance of a greased pig and Tomsoc made great fun of him, but when they were finished, Josh urged them all to pray for success and to add more wax over the summer so that the healing process would not fail. Josh would nurse the grafts through the summer heat, even fashioning small canopies to shade the wounds.

After the bruising work of tilling the grudging Vermont soil and the spring planting, the summer wore on with a blessed gentleness. The Acadians praised the bright, clear weather, which allowed them to ease up on the daily tasks and take their suppers by the lake. Many days ended thus and the idyllic sun up/sun down cycle seemed the perfect life. Josh felt himself putting down roots in this new country and nearly forgetting the coarseness of urban Boston. Rob coached Josh in the gentle art of yoking and driving oxen who after a number of humorous false starts, was geeing and hawing the animals with aplomb.

In the evenings, Josh and Rob, with Ian looking over their shoulders, would write passages from Josh's few books he had carried away from Boston. When Rob became frustrated and threatened to burn all his mistakes, Ian would place a heavy hand on his son's head, saying, "Steady lad. Josh is going to show you and me how a gentleman reads and writes." Before long, both MacKensies were scrawling rough sentences and haltingly reading some of Josh's simple exercises. The proud light in his friends' eyes were the only reward Josh wanted. Both Ian's friends and Amalie laughed and clapped loudly when, like magic, both students first wrote their names.

As the mild June evenings enveloped the little band of settlers, fireflies would come out of the dusk to mate, lighting the fields and forests with their silent beauty. Often clinging on their clothing, Josh and Tomsoc marveled at their number and elegance. Tomsoc, blending his native culture with Christianity, called them messengers of the Great Spirit who sent them to tell that peace would abide with all who saw them as evidence of His great plan. No Hair told them of the Moon Goddess who threw down to them pieces of her garment which the fireflies then gathered and knit back together in secret caves behind the mountains. On nights of summer lightning, the Moon Goddess gathered her new garment by fingers on forks of flame. She would wear this until the next year when she called upon the fireflies to weave her a new one. Basking in the storytelling, none of the settlement could guess that such a peaceful time would soon be cut asunder.

By mid-summer the first hay crop was ready for harvest and a bountiful one it was. The good weather held and the sturdy Acadians made short work of putting it safely in their barns. This left plenty of time to continue building Ian's inn and by late summer the roof went on. The fall harvest was next and all turned their labors to it. As Ian often told them, "There's two groaning seasons, spring and fall. We do all right if we don't let them weaken us!"

It had been a prosperous year. By late November, Ian and his family gathered all the Acadians for the harvest banquet. Other pioneers drifted in, welcomed by the Acadians. Even some scattered Native Americans skulked by to share the largess and company of their near kinfolk. This was not all generosity by Ian's band. The rough frontier living made such soirees vital bonding events to assure mutual survival when nature's challenges and hostile human depredations pressed the Acadians.

Infrequent travelers up the military road brought news fragments of Boston events. A Virginian named Washington had assumed command of Continental troops and surrounded the redcoats, but he and cooler heads knew that the farmer-militia was no match for a direct assault on the disciplined British. There was talk about colonial delegates in Philadelphia constructing some kind of declaration of freedom from King George and England. But not all were in favor of this. The group calling themselves Tories wanted no severance but an accommodation with the king and his ministers. Not much of this mattered to Josh or his newly adopted family. He assumed that the Barton brothers were changing their allegiances to fit the ironmongers market and hoped that their search for him was being lost in the turbulence of the rebellion.

9

KNOX
December 1775

By early December agricultural activities were curtailed as fodder and human food was put away for winter's siege. The inn was weatherproofed and Josh and Tomsoc were given a room in trade for seeing that the building was secure and ready for any travelers. Almost immediately there was a small party who would have the honor of christening the structure. A young bookseller out of Boston named Henry Knox, his bother, William, and several attendants arrived from a grueling ride up the Hudson via the city of New York on their way to Fort Ti. Knox was a huge man, estimated by Josh at nearly 25 stone. He and Tomsoc made sure that the crude bed for the man was properly reinforced. At supper, he explained his presence. Although a book vendor, General Washington had appointed him colonel of artillery and Ian quickly noted Knox's encyclopedic knowledge of warfare.

In close proximity at table, the curious Knox inquired about Josh's unusual neck scars and winced at the lad's tale of branding by the Boston Bartons. "Aye, as if the lobsterbacks aren't our only problem, we have scoundrels such as those among us." After supper, Knox got down to business. He had been sent to remove the cannon from Crown Point and Ticonderoga and transport them by sled to Boston. He needed both men and beasts to achieve this monumental task, moving down to Albany and the Hudson River, then east across the barrier known as the Berkshire Hills to Worcester and finally Boston where Washington would use them to close the siege on the redcoats.

"It's hard enough to move cannon in the dry season and you want to do it now?" Ian cried in disbelief.

"We don't have any choice. These are the type of guns we need and time is very short. Our minutemen may be fine militia, but to keep them shivering outside of Boston saps their morale and many of them will soon be at the end of their enlistments. There's much talk about getting home to prepare for spring planting."

"Then why don't you take the shorter route using the military road back to the Connecticut River and save time?"

Knox grinned and wiped his mouth. "Benedict Arnold recently came up here over that track. Too many mountains and too many wildernesses, he says. It would be slow going and men and beasts need food and shelter. Oxen can't be found in those Green Mountains and there's nothing to replace them when they tire or go lame. Besides, if the weather holds, we can float those cannons down the lake to the flat land round Albany and follow the river through the Dutch country. We'll be in civilization till we head across the Barrier."

While conversing, Knox put away a mountain of food. Just when it was time for desert, he cast an eye on the turkey drumstick left on the trencher. Rob pushed it to him, his face expressing awe. Ian sort of winced, knowing that his profit on this guest was going to be small. But when Knox asked if there were yokes of oxen that farmers wished to lease to him for the portage, Ian's eyes lit. He knew that the little Acadian settlement had seven yokes of sturdy French cattle that had little to do but lounge until spring.

Knox proposed a generous payment and Ian accepted. He would arrange terms with his Acadians the very next morning. With Ian's grudging assent, Rob and Josh would join the expedition. By sunset the following day, the seven yokes of newly shod oxen stood at the inn for Knox's inspection. Six drivers plus Rob and Josh would accompany them as far as Albany where other yokes, as needed, would be leased for the haul down the Hudson. Another exchange would be made in the Berkshires for the portage over the Barrier and to Boston.

Despite a chilling wind barreling down Champlain towards Fort Ti, the weather continued favorable as the little caravan of ox carts and men made their way to the fort. Other local farmers joined them as Rob, Josh and the Acadians drove their small phalanx of oxen through the huge wooden gate into the fort's parade ground. There a party of Green Mountain boys had already moved some lighter weapons from Crown Point fifteen miles to the north and had stripped Fort Ti's cannon off the old French-built carriages which were showing various stages of decay. Knox was already there, strutting about, his stentorian voice and bulky frame easily recognized even among the burley farmers. After giving a brief overview of what the expedition entailed, he asked the silent throng for questions. No one spoke, but Rob knew that they would gladly put up with this Bostonian colonel so long as he put real money in their pockets. Once contracted, the accompanying contingent of Green Mountain boys would both protect them and make sure none decided to take their cattle and skedaddle back home.

Loading the 60 cannons and mortars onto the carts was a Herculean task, but the farmers were equal to the effort and their freight was soon rumbling through Lower Falls village to the waiting boats. Here they were off-loaded and heaved onto the vessels for the short water trip around the Ticonderoga peninsula to Lake George. Again the ox carts were loaded to complete the three-mile portage to the Lake George landing, where another transfer to scows, pirogue and bateau would assure final water travel of 30 miles to Fort George at the south end of the lake. Time was not on their side as any day could bring harsh temperatures certain to freeze the lake and threaten failure for the entire venture. But with only minor mishaps, the cargo reached Fort George in a few days. Then it was reload the guns onto ox carts again and head for Albany via Fort Edward. Now Knox wished the hard freeze would come to facilitate travel over the primitive road. But the mild weather held. The ox carts made deep muddy ruts, slowing progress. A warm drizzle rain didn't help, rendering the narrow passage greasy and treacherous. As they neared Fort Edward, the caravan came upon a horse-drawn carriage that had skittered off the road and smashed a wheel. A family of well-dressed travelers stood in the muck surveying their misfortune while the driver, who had unhitched the horses, stood nearby calming his team. Knox cantered up on his steed and ordered Rob and Josh to repair the carriage with some of the extra supplies each oxcart carried just for such emergencies. The cannon caravan would continue on to Fort Edward and wait for them to catch up. As the gun carriages slogged past, one of the Green Mountain troops grunted under his breath, "Damn Tories. Good enough for "em!"

Three Tory women had remained in the carriage not wanting to soil their garments in the mud. Rob and Josh maneuvered the oxcart so the women could transfer onto it without touching the ground. Rob stood in the muck to catch each one should a slip occur. The last of the trio was a pretty girl of near 17 years who, according to Josh's recollection and banter, had her eyes fixed on Rob during most of the repair. With the women safely on the oxcart, Josh hitched his beasts to the carriage and pulled it back onto the road. Using levers and brawn, the two young men were able to remove the broken wheel, repair it and remount it in a matter of hours. Rob noted the name of the travelers on a chest strapped to the rear of the carriage. "Rev. Phineas Blair." The Reverend, a pleasant chap, introduced himself as the work got under way and also introduced his family, Mrs. Blair, their fetching older daughter, Jenny and the watchful younger daughter, Phoebe. "And who am I most obliged to for this help?", he queried. Rob mumbled his name that the Reverend repeated loudly to the women. "MacKensie, you say? Now here is a good Scots lad, ladies!" Looking at Josh, he waited for a response, but Josh just shrugged, feigning shyness, then blurted out, "Josh", not wanting to advertise.

The grateful travelers offered money, but the young men refused and the carriage continued on its way north towards Fort Anne. Reunited at Fort Edward, the artillery train continued south towards Albany. No one would have guessed then that in fewer two years hence another caravan, this time of lobsterbacks, would use the same rutted road in an attempt to split the New England colonies.

Most of Knox's artillery train had arrived at Albany before Christmas. Thanks to Dutch hospitality, the drivers and their escort were well cared for and the Knoxes and servant enjoyed their best meal since leaving the Acadian settlement. But there was no time to waste. Washington needed those cannons. January 1776 swept in cold and snowy as Knox rubbed his hands together more from satisfaction than from the icy blasts out of the Catskill Mountains to the west. "This hard freeze is just what we need, boys", he chortled as the Vermont ox teams were released and new ones added. He eyed the guns now being secured on sledges. "You lads over there", he continued, addressing Rob and Josh, "I'd like you to stay with me for the rest of the trip. What say, you?"

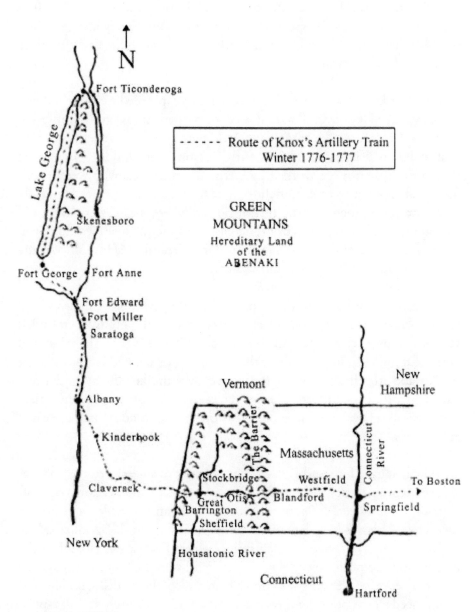

map by WHL

The boys looked at each other. "You'll be well paid and I need you. Your cattle are in the best of shape and you can send them back to Vermont with the other drivers. I'll assign you new teams." It took the two only minutes to say that they would be going to Boston with Knox. They assigned their beasts to their fellow Acadians along with the message to Ian that they were staying with the caravan.

The artillery train picked up speed now, proceeding south down the Hudson valley over flat and well-worn paths. Josh was impressed with the large Dutch patroon land holdings, sprinkled generously with well-maintained farms and barns fairly bursting with fodder. He learned that most of them were worked by German immigrants who were tenant farmers, beholden to their Dutch masters for seed and livestock. But only when the young men saw the manor houses where the masters lived, did they appreciate the vast wealth of the patroon system. "Josh, wouldn't you like to farm some of this land", Rob muttered dreamily? "Humph" was the reply. "Be careful what you wish for, my friend."

Late one afternoon as they approached the town of Kinderhook, a furious snowstorm swept out of the Catskills, over the Hudson and piled several feet on the cortege and their escort. Knox eyed the situation and decided to hole up in town until the storm ran its course. Despite the fat of the land, the hospitality of the natives was unlike Albany and Knox paid dearly for his comforts. It seemed clear that the procession's notoriety preceded its arrival and rates for harborage and fodder had increased accordingly.

The halt gave Josh and Rob the opportunity to shoe the oxen. Rob was an experienced farrier, having lived all his life with the necessity of draft animals. While oxen are generally more docile and durable than horses, their cloven hooves have less purchase on snowy ground. By shoeing, the feet of oxen are converted on their split platform by cleats to give a broader base with more push power. The train would soon be coming up against The Barrier, a challenging height of land called the Berkshire Hills and would need all the power and traction that could be mustered. Rob tapped in the shoe nails close to the outer rim of the hoof, carefully avoiding the sensitive interior of the cleft

10

Proceeding down the valley from Kinderhook, the Green Mountain boys couldn't help noticing that a small group of mounted men were shadowing the train. All were richly dressed and rode well fed and groomed horses. But Knox took no notice and by the time they reached Claverack, the riders had disappeared. After bedding the oxen down for the night in a sturdy lean-to, Rob and Josh joined Knox at the inn for supper. While putting down his usual huge complement of chicken and gravy, he asked the young men if the beasts were ready for the trip east in the morning.

"Never seen oxen in better shape," Rob responded. Knox grinned and cautioned the lads to watch carefully from now on, as the trip would be more challenging over the hills. Josh nodded in exhaustion as he finished apple pie, indicating to Rob that he was bushed from the day's journey. He left immediately to bed down in the straw loft above the cattle.

He'd just gotten comfortable when a hand touched his shoulder. He swiftly rolled left and rose to a crouch, ready for an assailant. "Easy!", came the soft voice of Tomsoc.

Shaking off terror, Josh whispered. "You sure scared me. What are you doing here?"

"Ian sent me to stay with you and Rob. He didn't want two young lads spoiling themselves in Albany town and now I find that you will go on to Boston. All the more reason to keep you out of trouble."

Josh was stung with resentment to think he needed watching, but was genuinely glad to see Tomsoc.

"You better get some food, Tomsoc. There was lots left at the inn. You stay here and I'll go so they won't give you trouble."

Josh slogged back to the inn through a foot of snow. Out beyond the stables for the beasts he could see the sleds with their cannon standing next to the road. There was movement out there with several mounted riders moving slowly by the weapons. It was dark, except for the glow of candles in windows, but local folk were still about making their way home and he thought of nothing but getting his friend some food and returning to the warmth of the loft.

Tomsoc heard the crunch of feet nearing the cowshed. Not one set, but several and his caution kicked in. Suddenly two figures appeared below him carrying a third who was thoroughly bound and gagged. After throwing their burden, writhing and whimpering, onto some straw, they dashed back out into the night. Tomsoc was on his feet and down the ladder in a flash. When he saw the fear in the bound man's eyes, he knew he'd better not release him. He was one of the Green Mountain boys protecting the artillery train and feared the savages and their knives more than Old Harry himself.

Looking out to the weapons, Tomsoc saw two horsemen milling about, holding the mounts of the two whom had dispatched the guard. They were busy examining the cannons and discussing their strategy in low tones. It didn't take Tomsoc long to cover the ground to the first horse and grab the bit in the animal's teeth. The creature reared back frightened by this intruder, but the Indian held fast.

"What the Hell?", was the confused reaction from the rider as he tried to steer away from this surprise. In the dark it was difficult to discern what was happening, but the two on the ground quickly abandoned the cannons and remounted. One of them, closer to the horse now controlled by Tomsoc, drew a heavy pistol and struck the Indian with the butt. Tomsoc saw flashing light, but still clung tightly, until a second blow sent him sprawling in the snow.

Josh left the back entry to the inn with Tomsoc's food and immediately came upon the melee. He let out a hoot as four riders flashed past him and galloped down the Rhinebek Road. He was soon joined by more of the Green Mountain contingent who found Tomsoc sore and shaken, but whole. They wanted to dispatch him right away when they found their colleague in the lean-to, but the released guard explained that the Indian had nothing to do with his capture and Josh's spirited defense of his friend warded them off.

Next morning, Knox examined the scene. Several rods and a hammer were found in the snow among the hoof prints and he correctly concluded that the raid was by someone wanting to spike the guns.

"All you have to do is pound one of these spikes into the touchhole and the cannon is ruined. It can never be fired again. We'd better check every piece for tampering."

The check revealed nothing and Tomsoc was suddenly elevated to special status in Knox's book. The Green Mountain Boys were not so enthusiastic, but grudgingly accepted, especially since one of their own had been surprised and overcome.

"Knew we could never trust these Yorkers. They been after our land for years and want the King to protect them," the more vocal of the group cried.

Knox gave them a level eye. "That may be so, but there're more than Yorkers who want to stay with the King. See that rocky, domed mountain to our right, there," he said, pointing. "T'other side of that is Connecticut and it's full of King lovers. Before this battle is over, we're going to find that we have lots of Tories among us, some of them your neighbors."

They started immediately on a line that would ultimately take them to Boston, some 150 miles away as the crow flies. Knox was jovial. "We're on the homestretch, boys. And the fun is just beginning." he chortled. The flatland running along the Hudson soon gave way to undulating hills. In the distance, drawing closer with each mile were the white capped lumps of the Barrier.

They crossed the Bay Colony border at Egremont, a cluster of four farmhouses, standing forlornly in the cold, but lined with the curious from surrounding farms, all wanting to see the artillery train. First settled by a few Dutch, this land now, by right of possession, belonged to hard-working yeoman English. Word was spreading fast of the expedition and was being more warmly welcomed by these rural folk as it penetrated deeper and deeper into Massachusetts. These English had long sparred with the Yorker poltroons and Crown magistrates in ways similar to the Green Mountain Boys. Less than two years before they had driven the Royal judges from their chambers in the town they now approached.

Great Barrington proved to be a congenial place despite the challenging Berkshire Hills weather. Situated on the lovely river bearing its former name, Housatonik, Mohican for "over the mountain", it was the eastern terminus for the former fur trade route to the Hudson and Albany. Going east over the Barrier the route petered out almost immediately into a very rough track. Most trade and commerce was tied to the Hudson despite social and ethnic differences and few traveled the track east save the occasional body of soldiery. This left the settlers of the Housatonik rather isolated and dependent on each other for support rather than outsiders, a circumstance in which they saw as no disadvantage and had learned to cherish.

11

Knox liked the hospitality he found in Great Barrington and tarried long after the oxen were exchanged and new drivers assigned. Like the Dutch at an earlier time, he admired the flat, fertile floodplain of the Housatonik River that lay embraced by rolling, forested hills. Musing at table, he announced to Rob and Josh that he would invest here had not his ties to Boston and land in Maine locked in his limited capital. Remembering Boston's fetid air and squalor, this thought was not lost on Josh, who, though penniless, agreed that the valley's beauty and isolation had much promise.

By mid-January the train finally moved over the Housatonik and started for Three-Mile Hill. Although the now rolling landscape was a bit rougher than the Hudson plains, the Berkshire barrier seemed a midget compared to their northern Green Mountain cousins. Rob and Josh chuckled as the reputed "hill" was not to be seen. Off to the north was an imposing rock face that they incorrectly assumed was their goal. "Hell, no", a local driver grumbled. "That'll be Squaw Peak. Only a damn fool would try to lug cannons up there." Sure enough, a little way out of town, their route shifted right and they plodded several miles across a flat plain.

Rob nudged Josh. "These folks sure have a funny sense of humor. No challenging barriers out this way."

In less than an hour, their smirks disappeared as they confronted a short, sharp rise through an eroded gash cut between two slabs of granite. There was no stopping as the drivers urged their beasts into the climb. The first small cannons made it to the top, but two of the larger sleds nearly skidded off over an edge which dropped close to twenty feet into a frozen brook.

Rob unhitched and brought a set of oxen back to help the straining pair, then another pair before they managed to save both cannons and beasts. Finally besting this obstacle, the train continued on, slow-going through a snowbound pine forest, the track ever coiling and gaining elevation up East Mountain. By dark they had reached an isolated farm consisting of a cottage and several small lean-tos, the only sign of civilization that afternoon. The cluster sat in a stump forest and anyone could see that cattle fodder and human sustenance was mighty scarce in these hardscrabble surroundings. Knox sized up the situation and not wanting to over-exert the oxen, decided to spend the night after learning that four miles further was an inn where his troops might get a meager meal. While Rob and Josh remained to settle the oxen, Knox sent his troops and drivers in small group rotations to the inn. Then the three had a spare meal with the farm family, gathering as much information as they could on the conditions of the track eastward.

An east wind blowing heavy snow in squalls all afternoon made Rob nervous. He had seen winds coming over the lake from the Adirondacks act the same way, then dump their heavy load in several hours, making passage even between farm buildings nearly impossible. Knox, a Maine man, scoffed. He knew all about northeasters.

"These Berkshires are too far from the coast and isolated for that", he laughed. Rob wasn't so sure and Tomsoc, ever skeptical, but guarded, remained stoical. The next morning seemed to prove Knox right. Winds had shifted south and grew warm, melting away what had fallen. Knox was in high spirits as they hitched up.

"We'll make many miles today, so let's move along now, boys."

By afternoon, even Knox was casting malevolent glances at the sky. The track was hard to follow and the oxen slowed way down as their hooves continually broke through the thin ice of the endless bogs and swales. Rounding a bend, the rugged track simply stopped and they knew a wrong turn had been taken. Dark was coming on fast as Knox sent several horsemen back to see where they had gone astray. The train turned around and retraced their path until dark when Knox called a halt and broke the bad news that they would overnight in a nearby copse of hemlock. This gave them some protection from the wind which now blew harder than ever, at times with gale force, the snow squalls becoming lasting and heavy. Snow was piling up fast and the driving flakes were obscuring vision. The drivers cut away lower branches of the firs to create a small, snow-free haven for the animals. The slash was used for firewood and soon hot, popping flames illuminated the lost band. Tomsoc showed them how to make an Indian brush shelter, a makeshift lean-to with limbs and boughs for a roof which was then heaped with snow, the opening facing away from the driving snow. It was hardtack and jerky for supper, gifts generously supplied by their hosts in Great Barrington.

About midnight the reconnoiters returned. They had found the right path and had reached the tiny hamlet of Otis whose outstanding feature was a wilderness inn. By a happy circumstance, the horsemen brought back several barrels of hard cider that Knox magnanimously distributed to the men, keeping a sizeable portion for himself. Everyone was dog-tired from slogging through the wet snow, but Knox, voice booming, regaled the drivers until early morning with song and laughter, becoming more ribald as his cider supply diminished.

He surprised them all by arising at first light and after hurrying everyone through hardtack and melted snow had the train moving swiftly out of the copse. The storm had abated at dawn and the extra snow now greased the runners of the gun carriages, much to the delight of the drivers. Soon they were passing the inn. Knox lifted his hat to the owner and his family whose eyes were agog at the weaponry and the Vermont militia.

Later in the afternoon, the train suddenly slid over a hill that looked down on another tiny hamlet. Knox whipped out his maps and scratched his head. Something was not right. He sent a rider down into the settlement for information and learned that he was in Sandisfield, considerably off course. To continue would take the guns into Connecticut, hardly a welcome destination. Cursing vehemently, Knox chucked his maps into a saddlebag and stomped off in a blue funk. The beasts stood still, waiting for their next direction. The drivers leaned on their sleds in silence. Knox was not one to cross when in this mood. Finally, he came up to Rob and Josh who briefly thought that the commander would take out his frustration on them. But his sudden smile told them otherwise. "Better turn your yokes ass end to, boys. We're going back again. Washington will just have to be patient, eh?" His jovial laugh took the strain off the entire train as they turned back up the trail.

Two days later, after stumbling through what seemed to Josh and Rob an impenetrable woods of rolling hills, hollows, bogs and icy valleys, a point man on horseback returned to tell Knox that he'd run into a group of men who could barely speak English and weren't overly friendly. Knox frowned, as he had hoped that his next stop would be a welcome one where they could safely shelter and feed their beasts. An hour later, these rough-hewn folks, armed with muskets, stood blocking the trail, facing the train with grim expressions. It wasn't until Knox greeted them with Rob by his side that tensions eased. As soon as one had opened his mouth, Rob recognized the dialect as Gaelic Scots. Ian MacKensie may have absorbed the French of the Acadians, but still used much of the Scots dialect that had been bred into him. Earlier on, a group of immigrants from the old country had pioneered these Barrier hills to the west of the Connecticut River and built a community called Blandford. Separated from colonial contacts, they kept their speech patterns and rarely communed with the flatlanders of the Connecticut River valley. To Knox's surprise, Rob had no trouble understanding these taciturn farmers.

Knox also breathed a sigh of relief, knowing from his crude maps that the way to Boston would no longer be climbing hills. The train slid into the little hamlet where Knox again commandeered a spot at the rustic inn run by an English-speaking family from Yorkshire called Hayden. Reserved and of few words, they at least spoke in a tongue he could understand, provided decent fare and the first real bed Knox had seen since crossing the Housatonik. Coming out of his shell a bit, proprietor Hayden shared that his son was among the Continentals at Boston. He also warned that the trip down to Westfield wouldn't be easy and offered to rouse a team of farmers in the morning to guide the train over some tricky downslopes, if that would help the colonial cause. Knox welcomed the idea and turned in early to sleep comfortably. The drivers, their teams and the Green Mountain boys were billeted in a barn behind the inn and after a substantial inn meal, created nests in the dry hay of the loft savoring the body heat of their beasts below.

The trip down the eastern slope of the Barrier proved to be nearly as difficult as the wilderness trek up from Great Barrington. But Hayden's guides knew every turn and switchback and provided the needed navigation required to keep the weapons' sledges from pushing the teams and drivers into the many boulder-lined ravines. Ropes and safety chains were fixed to trees uphill and to each sled before it was allowed to descend the steeper gradients. Knox was most relieved when the Westfield flatlands hove into sight. Washington would now soon have his guns.

At Springfield the artillery train oxen were exchanged for speedier horsepower. Tomsoc remained with the oxen, now relieved of their functions. Noting that the rest of the expedition would be less challenging, his friends convinced him to proceed north up the Connecticut River Valley to Fort #4 to await there for their arrival from Boston. The artillery train would now snake on easily over the post road across central Massachusetts. Approaching Cambridge, the towns were many and crowds lined the road, each assemblage giving rousing cheers to Knox and his company. Josh and Rob became charged with the euphoria and accepted cakes and sweet cider drinks by the score. Knox kept stern watch to be sure all his troops stayed in line and that no one got pie-eyed with hard stuff. A large color guard headed by Washington himself came out to meet them. Knox bowed graciously and turned the cannons over to the waiting militia. Formalities done, the train personnel billeted their teams and were dismissed while Knox retired to Washington's headquarters, but not before he quietly cautioned Josh to beware of bounty hunters looking for escaped servants.

*　　*　　*

Colonel Arnold was in trouble. The long march through the Maine woods and up unknown streams as depicted on faulty maps had reduced his small army to tatters. Even with Montgomery's successful capture of Montreal and drive up the St Lawrence River to Quebec, the combined force had failed to take the citadel. Montgomery was mowed down in an early fusillade, Arnold himself wounded and the colonial forces decimated by hunger, cold and disease. The retreat beside the St. Lawrence, back through the Quebec flatlands and down the Richelieu River to Champlain was bitter. Most discouraging was the fact that the French had not risen in revolt as expected. Dreams of a 14th colony to support the War for Independence were dashed and the gateway to New England was wide open.

Now, as was his nature, Arnold brooded alone on Ticonderoga's battlements, the harsh winter wind from Canada in his face, his eyes tearing, the foot wound painful and pounding. He so missed his Margaret, now moldering in a Connecticut grave. "What next?", he muttered darkly to himself.

Over the Green Mountains in Windsor, Ethan Allen and others were debating how to take advantage of opportunities this conflict provided. A separate territory of Vermont would eliminate at last the incursions of the Yorkers and contacts with the British seemed to assure the venture of Crown support. These hardscrabble farmers also didn't care much for the Boston dandies showing up to take over and telling them what to do. Most delegates were calling for an independent Vermont republic. By January 1777, they would have it, including universal suffrage for men, and other freedoms unheard of in the rebel 13 colonies or even in Mother England. The long-sought 14th colony would finally emerge, but stand by itself.

12

Cambridge 1776

The Cambridge encampment was huge, but amorphous, with a wide range of uniforms and farmers' garb moving hither and yon in no particular order. Josh and Rob soon concluded that the color guard was just a showpiece. Some units were at close order drill while others just lounged, guffawing loudly when the raw recruits became lost in a maze of unclear commands. Toward sunset, cooking fires were begun to prepare the evening meal. Each unit had its own larder, ample or slim, depending on the generosity of and distance of travel to the towns sending men to Washington's army. Not surprising, the disparity fomented conflicts between units and dampened esprit that had been so evident the previous April. Short-term enlistments were running out and some men were even now packing up to depart for home and spring planting. The siege cannons would help to further discourage the British in Boston, but this colonial army was fast coming unglued.

Food and darkness quelled the cacophony of milling soldiers. The officers retired to dinner, drinks and gossip at the local inns and a hush settled on the encampment. Knox saw that Rob and Josh shared the food of the generous contingent of Minutemen from nearby Quincy. "Courtesy of my friend, Mr. John Adams." he remarked slyly. Upon finishing supper, a solitary horn blew from the picket line overlooking the neck of land leading out of Boston. Several Minutemen smiled, picked up their gear and left.

"Where are they off to?" Rob asked the soldier nearby. All he got was a smirk and a shrug, but a sergeant across the fire circle blurted out, "They be the women coming."

The sergeant lead them to the picket line and pointed downward. A small cluster of figures was slowly approaching the encampment, led by a man on horseback. "There be the prostitutes", the sergeant stated matter-of-factly. "They come out every night to serve the troops and take what few shillings they can get. Every army has them, but these here get the trade both sides, lobsterbacks and continentals."

As the figures came closer, soldiers began to line up behind Rob and Josh. The sargeant chuckled. "Unless you plan on making a purchase, you better get out of the way for these fellers."

Rob and Josh stepped back as a soldier approached carrying a torch. They could now make out the women's faces. Some were old and lined, but many were fresh and a few appeared fetching. The waiting soldiers jostled for better position to proposition the latter. In the flickering light, they could see the women smiling provocatively, often showing a gaping hole where their front teeth should have been. As the torchbearer moved closer to illuminate the women, the man leading the group, rode his horse to cut him off. In the sudden flash of light, Josh was struck dumb and quickly shielded his face, moving slowly backward into the dark. The horseman was no other than Justice.

"No business here 'til I gets mine", he roared and extracted a basket from behind his saddle in which purchasers were to drop money before passing. Josh could hear the coins clinking fast and furious as Justice let them pass among the women. "That old devil.'" Josh said to himself. "Running a flesh trade right under the nose of two hostile armies."

Josh continued to melt into the dark and the assembling soldiers. Rob caught up with him and asked what his hurry was. "That picaroon creature on the horse knows that I'm missing from the Barton's slave shop. I can't have him find me here or he'll have the Bartons drag me back. I'm sure he was too busy with his taking money to have recognized me."

Rob thought for a time, repelled both by what they were seeing and by the abusive system of English indenture.

"Let's get out of here'" he spat out and turned to retrace steps back to the campfire.

Later that night, Rob and Josh made their beds on straw next to the tethered oxen, grateful for the body warmth of the huge beasts. But Josh was not sleeping. He was too close to Boston for comfort and now that the artillery was delivered, it was time to return to Champlain. He rose to relieve himself, but had barely left the makeshift lean-to when an iron hand closed on his neck.

"Remember me, Dogshit?"

Josh struggled, but try as he might, he was unable to break the grip. He did manage to knock a grain measure onto Rob asleep nearby who mumbled "What the devil?", only half awake. Spotting the stranger, he sprang up meaning to free Josh, but found himself looking into the business end of an ugly dagger.

"Another step and your friend here is a dead soldier." He smiled malevolently. "Thought he'd steal my money when I wasn't looking."

"Let him go.", Rob growled. "He stole nothing and I can prove it."

"Then what's that there laying at his feet?"

Rob looked down and saw a sack of coins on the straw, cleverly dropped by Justice as cover for his invasion. Rob stooped and picked it up, handing it to Justice, saying, "Here, take it and get on your way." Justice showed his yellowed front teeth. "Won't be that easy. My friends in Boston will pay well to have this scum back. He's goin' with me, so throw that purse here and stand back." Rob complied, but out of the dark loomed the Quincy sargeant. Justice suddenly went on the defensive, repeating his charge of theft and began to back out of the lean-to with Josh in tow.

"We'll let the tribunal decide this." The sargeant grasped the purse and ordered Justice to unhand Josh. The eyes flickered and the teeth appeared once more as Justice sheathed his knife. They all appeared that very night before one of Washingon's cobbled together tribunals to hear and resolve altercations between militia men. A major and two lieutenants sitting at a table in one of the local inns heard them out. The major appeared uncomfortable and when he learned that neither Josh nor Justice had any standing with the army, dismissed the case and ordered them out. Justice thought he had won, but as he led Josh away to his women, Rob ran to the inn where he knew Knox was residing, broke in on his supper and told him the story. Knox scowled and motioned to the captain in charge of security for the artillery train. A short time later, Rob and the captain found Justice mounting up with Josh tethered along side. Brandishing a pistol. The captain ordered Justice to dismount, free Josh and hand over the sack of coins. Swearing heatedly, he reluctantly obeyed, turning an evil eye on Rob and newly freed Josh. Holding the horse's reins, the captain told Justice to join his female retinue and get the hell out of Cambridge. The tribunal major suddenly appeared with a small contingent of troops and urged captain, horse and the two friends to return to Knox at the inn. As they departed, Rob looked back to see the major huddling with Justice and calling for several carriages to carry him and his friends back into Boston. "Funny way to treat that old scoundrel.", he remarked to his friend. "Indeed", muttered Josh.

Next morning, Knox called them both to the inn. "Didn't know that you were such a valuable runaway, Josh. With a price on your head, your owners will be out here in a flash when word gets to them. You've got to leave this place at once. Take this purse and that old devil's horse and go. We don't know who you are or where you went, but with those burns on your hide they'll find you quick if you stay here."

Rob and Josh looked at each other. Rob nodded that Josh had better leave, saying he'd make his way back with the Green Mountain men. As Josh rode away north up the road to Concord and beyond where he would join Tomsoc, Rob joined the other drivers. Knox and the major reported to General Washington.

"I don't trust that old reprobate, sir," Knox reported to the general. "Your aide-de-camp, Major Jennings here handled this latest fracas well, but it seems every time old Justice gives us information on the British, he gets into trouble."

Washington pursed his lips. "Not much we can do about it, Henry. Justice gets valuable intelligence from his trollops and while I don't like to see him or them around here, they provide a perfect cover for him to tell us what Howe is up to."

"You are right, of course, sir, but might he take back to Boston things about us that Howe shouldn't know?"

"Are you suggesting that he is a double agent?"

"Not sure, but he's a slippery old cuss."

"The news of your arrival with the cannons is just what I want Howe to know, Henry. It may hasten his departure when he sees them on Dorchester Heights and realizes what they can do to his ships. Then we'll have the upper hand." He turned to Jennings. "By the way, did you treat him well, Major?"

"Yes sir. He was paid handsomely and even took away two carriages worth far more than the horse he lost."

"Very good, gentlemen. Let's keep all of this quiet. If Howe decides to leave soon, we may be able to keep what's left of the continental army in arms for however the British decide to confront us next. And you can be sure that they will. Word from Quebec is that Arnold wasn't successful. This war may turn out to be a long one."

Without the redcoats' knowledge, the cannon were placed on Dorchester Heights in the dark of night, a feat nearly as astounding as their movement from Fort Ti. Two weeks later a rousing cheer went up from the Continental Army as Washington and Knox watched the British clamber onto Howe's ships waiting in Boston Harbor for evacuation to Halifax, Nova Scotia. Boston would never see lobsterbacks again.

13

Spring came late to Champlain in 1776. Ever industrious, the Acadian farmers adapted to the weather and were putting seed in the ground even as a late dusting of snow mantled their fields. "Poor man's fertilizer", they joked as they rubbed down their animals after the day's work. As brighter evenings grew longer, Rob, assisted by Josh, broadened his reading from the cache of books that Knox had given Rob prior to his departure for home. News reaching the tiny settlement was often old by the time it arrived. The two friends quickly devoured printed news and broadsides obtained once a month in Skenesboro. Even old Ian kept up with the colonial turmoil, but with a jaundiced eye, ever suspicious of both Tories and the so-called Rebels.

Amalie Hebert, daughter of one of the original Acadian settlers, was a quick study. Petite, but healthy as a horse, she shouldered more than her share of the daily tasks at age sixteen. She and Rob had known each other since childhood and many thought that their friendship would soon become matrimonial. Yet, regardless of teasing by the other eligible women who were more than slightly jealous, they both denied these fanciful predictions. Whenever she could, Amalie hung around Josh and Rob, as a gleeful gadfly, quietly absorbing information and soon was conversing haltingly in English and writing both her name and simple sentences. Before long, she became the conduit for the rest of the Acadian women to keep them apprised of all the rumblings to their south.

Skenesboro was fast becoming a military focal point in the Champlain Valley. Settled after the French and Indian War by a former British Army officer, Captain Philip Skene, it occupied the very southern tip of Lake Champlain and served as a tiny port and transfer site for American and

Canadian goods moving up and down the lake. Connected by a passable southerly road to Forts Anne and Edwards, it also linked trade to Albany and the Hudson River. Besides his trade connections, Skene developed a sawmill and gristmill and had built himself a stately fieldstone home to become a colonial mogul overseeing his many acres, a gift from the King of England. This connection and hard-core Tory support gave him considerable influence in the area. Not surprising then, that in 1775 a contingent of Green Mountain boys captured Skenesboro and relieved him of this responsibility shortly after Ticonderoga fell. Skene was away on business in England and this violation raised the ire of other Tories residing in the area, including the Reverend Phineas Blair. As a group, the Tories more often than not were educated, wealthy and had firm ties to the motherland. The rebels tolerated them as the colonial revolt churned on, largely because their influence and money would be a boon if only they could be convinced to join the cause.

The booty of this takeover included Skene's trading schooner which was promptly armed, renamed the "Liberty" and commandeered by Benedict Arnold for a minor, but successful raid down the Richelieu River on Fort St. Johns, Quebec. This did nothing to blunt Arnold's fame when he reported to General Washington in Boston and certainly was not overlooked by British military strategists seeking to protect Canada and, by force of arms, to split open and isolate New England from the rest of the rebel colonies.

The maple syrup season waned as warm breezes popped out the maple buds. Ice remained in the lakes and ponds, but the marshes began to surge with marigolds and skunk cabbage. Early bees were finding energy and sustenance here and melt water murmured in the brooks leading to the ponds. With the land awakening, preparations began to sow another year's crop. Mud season was about gone as the Acadians sought out whatever emerging wild, edible greens to supplement their dry, coarse fare of winter.

Rob and Amalie often scoured the margins of brooks searching for young, succulent fiddle-head ferns, Rob, armed with Ian's horse pistol, serving as shield against wild things, including army deserters and possible rouge travelers. As Amalie gathered, Rob related his tale of the artillery train and Boston. She missed nothing and drew out even small details by repeated questions, knowing that he was rather full of himself and his adventure. As evening drew on, they climbed a familiar ridge, which provided a lovely sunset vista and overlooked a huge marsh, once an arm of water leading out to the Champlain depths. Clambering up the rocky prominence, their ears caught the sudden cacophony of thousands of amphibian voices, the mating calls of spring peepers aroused from their winter sleep. The sound wafting up from the vale deep below the ridge and already in shadow was stunning as they rested on a boulder to watch the last few rays of the sun. From this vantage point, with trees not yet in new leaves, Rob could look to the east and see parts of the military road snaking on up towards Fort Ti. A distinct cleft in the far reaches of the ridge could be seen, the spot where Father Henri had met his fate. Called "the Notch", it was a feared place by the Acadians who stepped lively in making passage.

Tired from the gathering, Amalie leaned on his shoulder as she had done many times since their childhood and in no time the pail with the harvested fiddleheads slipped from her hands as she drifted off to sleep.

He held her close to be sure she, too, did not topple and did his best to make her comfortable. Then, for the first time, he noticed what she had been enduring. She had not complained once of the squadrons of blackflies, those mobile, blood-sucking female denizens which arose from swift-flowing streams and attacked anything warm-blooded, especially soft-skinned women. He pitied her the dozen red welts near her eyes and at the hairline, the blood still seeping from them and matting the hair strands to her skin. They should have gone back to the settlement long ago. All the while he had told his tales, he had overlooked this attack by tiny marauders.

As she relaxed in his embrace, he observed her flawless lips and cheeks. Her warmth and gentle breathing aroused him pleasantly. Her hands, like his, were roughened from peasant work and stained green from the ferns. Growing up, he and Amalie had been molded by the common community, but of late he had gradually become conflicted by what he knew was true. They were children no longer. Gently, he adjusted the collar of her outer garment against the cool drafts from the swamp and brushed a few bloody coils of hair away from her brow. Startled, she woke suddenly, quickly slid away from him and commenced gathering her spill, blushing unseen in the gathering dark. Neither remarked on the incident as they made their way home.

14

Caleb Elkinton, eldest son of one of Skenesboro's prominent Tories, rode casually through the village to Skene's gristmill. His purpose this spring morning was to clinch the annual contract with the miller for the Elkinton estate's grain crop. He had hopes for a fair bargain, but was no fool. Since the colonial takeover much had changed. Those who had been friends now avoided him, the continental broadsides circulating among the working folk having stirred them into unrest. What formerly were congenial rural gatherings were turning into glum, tight-lipped events, some degenerating into shouting and mob psychology. There was even talk of appropriating estate land for the purpose of supporting a New England army headed by that Virginian, Washington. The usual courtesy nods to his passage by townsfolk were now absent as he made his way towards the mill.

Inside the counting room he sat in negotiation with a sharp-eyed clerk from Boston who now had control of operations, replacing the elderly miller who stood forlornly by the door, dust-covered from his labor. The miller who shifted his eyes to the clerk did not meet Caleb's nod of recognition. "Not a good beginning", thought Caleb as he took a seat across from the clerk.

He opened by offering the same terms as the previous year, but it was soon apparent that the Bostonian would have none of that. He was offering a much lower amount and demanded delivery to the very door of the mill, something that had never been required in previous contracts. After extended haggling, they finally agreed on terms slightly below what Caleb wanted, but with no delivery. The clerk then closed his books rather rudely, clearly indicating that the session was ended. But there was more as the clerk leaned back and touching together the fingers of both hands gave Caleb an icy smile.

"You are aware, sir, that payment will be in continental currency?"

Caleb's jaw tightened. He hadn't expected this. His response was calm and measured.

"That is unacceptable. We both know that this new money is untested and probably worthless. I'll take nothing but coin of the realm."

The clerk now smiled more broadly, showing a blackened tooth. "You think you can sell in Albany for a better price? That will cost you considerable time, labor and travel. But you have my offer. We are done here."

Caleb rose and turned towards the miller who shrugged his shoulders and again refused to meet his eyes. Nor did he accompany Caleb to his horse at the hitching post, as was his habit in the past.

By the time Caleb entered the estate grounds, he had prepared in his mind the trip south. He knew he'd get a better deal with the Albany merchants, but there were other benefits as well to be gained in the lower Hudson valley where a corps of like-minded folk was organizing to oppose this overbearing rebel rabble.

Two weeks later, he met with a small group of Tories and British officers in a Rhinebek tavern. His role was to be keeping the British informed of rebel activity on the lakes and quietly recruiting battle-ready men for a Loyalist regiment.

*   *   *

Arnold chafed at what he was seeing at Ticonderoga. He knew that an army with nothing to do was a recipe for disaster. Any spirit and high morale generated by events of 1775 was being dissipated by garrison duty. Desertions were up and the quality of troops remaining was poor. Drunkeness was on the increase and even the officers were unreliable to enforce discipline, choosing to favor only those who had elected them to lead. Just when good weather arrived in May, informants from Quebec reported the construction of a sizeable British fleet at St. John. After the scare Arnold had given Quebec City in January, reinforcements had arrived from England, including a naval vessel, which had no equal on the lakes. The commander of these combatants, Colonel Guy Carleton, was busily preparing to move south.

Alarmed, Arnold quickly petitioned General Schuyler, the recently appointed military commander of the Champlain region, to construct gunboats to confront Carleton's force. Schuyler hesitated, but dispatched a rider to Boston with this information and a request for permission to proceed.

"My friend," Arnold addressed Schuyler, "do we really have time to wait on some committee's permission repel the British?"

"Now, Benedict, don't be hasty. We have no vessels, men or armaments for such a venture. We will wait and see what Carleton's force looks like, then confront him on land and at the narrows where the forts can rake his fleet."

Arnold, typically short on patience, growled "But . . . but."

Schuyler threw up his hands. "I'll hear no more!", he shouted, then added with a smile. "Should you wish to make some preparations to keep our boys busy, however, I shall look the other way."

Arnold immediately sprang into action. Without waiting for an answer from General Washington, he commenced to build his own flotilla of small ships. Skene's sawmill whined non-stop as lumber was cut during every hour of daylight. Carpenters were recruited from Vermont and Albany to cobble together whatever small-masted navy they could.

Sensing yet another opportunity for economic improvement, the Acadians hurriedly prepared their fields, then left for paid labor in Skenesboro, leaving the women to maintain their farms. Josh and Rob were among them, despite Ian's insistence that they not become involved in any more planned military activity. Tomsoc would stay with the women to help with the heavy lifting needed at the farms.

In Skenesboro, the two young men, now fully seasoned oxen drivers, joined the small army of woodsmen dragging white pine to the mill. Arnold was everywhere goading them on to complete his flotilla. By late summer more than a dozen vessels lay at the Skenesboro dock. They weren't much to look at, but each was lightly armed with small cannon and staffed with makeshift crews aching for a fight. Arnold recognized Josh and Rob among the woodsmen and did his best to sign them on for the fray, but they would not go back on their word to Ian.

After frenzied preparations for sailing downlake to the north, the gunboats shoved off none too soon, as word of the 30 vessel British fleet was underway south to attack Forts Ti and Crown Point. Josh and Rob saw them off at the dock and restrained themselves from joining the small band of observers going north on land by foot to witness the expected battle. It would not be hard to keep up with Arnold's fleet as it rowed past the forts and entered the wider expanses of Champlain. At a brief stop at Fort Ti, Arnold learned that the British ships had departed St. John and, weather permitting, would be within range of Crown Point in a matter of days. Wasting no time, he harried his rowers to greater speed and, taking advantage of a favorable breeze, sped on alone in the two-masted schooner, the USS Royal Savage. Rejecting the narrows at Chimney Point as undefendable against the larger British fleet, he pushed on north, trusting that his rowers would catch up before the British found him. He knew his popgun sailors were no match for the superior British firepower and carefully sought a stretch of water where the limited seamanship of his unskilled crews would not be tested. Scanning his rough map, he noted that given time and speed, the two combatants would meet near Valcour Island, a rocky nub with just enough room behind it to hide his little squadron. There he waited.

Caleb had seen enough of the summer activity at Skene's sawmill and the emerging Continental Navy. Weeks before Arnold sailed north, he had accompanied a group of Mohawk traders paddling up Champlain's eastern shore towards Canada. Information on this rag-tag, rebel fleet would be of great interest to Colonel Carleton in St. John.

Josh and Rob made ready to return home. While Josh packed their few belongings, Rob went into Skenesboro to purchase essentials for the tavern. Just before entering the dry goods store for a several bolts of bright cloth he knew would delight No Hair and the women in the settlement, he noticed a carriage proceeding slowly towards him. At the window flew a small banner of cloth just the color he was thinking of for the women. The carriage pulled to a stop and a young woman emerged. Rob immediately recognized her as the one he had lifted from the damaged carriage on the road to Fort Anne. She caught his eye and smiled, a faint blush rising in her cheeks. Rob nodded his welcome with a tip of his peasant cap and extended a hand to help her up the rough steps of the store.

"Thank you. Sir." The voice was soft, calm, and cultured, a sound he rarely heard. "And thank you for the repair of our carriage on the road to the forts."

Rob nodded again, pleased that she had remembered. "My pleasure to see you again and to know that your carriage is still good." He tried to mask his Acadian accent to no avail.

She preceded him into the store as he took notice of her slender neck and arms, the fine styling of hair under a pristine bonnet. Unashamedly, he wondered about the swell of her breasts in the fine dress and what was under it propelling her gracefully among the displays. When she cast an eye towards him, he looked quickly away, but not before realizing that she must have felt his gaze. When they came near each other next to a display, she addressed him directly, holding out a gloved hand.

"My name is Phoebe Blair." Rob stumbled for something more to say and finally blurted out, "I'm Robert MacKensie, just looking here for some fabric for the women back home." He was again mortified by the sound of his Acadian accent and busied himself among the fabrics.

"Ah, yes, I remember my father's noting your name on the road. And where is home, Rob?"

"Over in the Green Mountains, near Castleton. Been working the woods here for the boatbuilders," he mumbled, then straightened up and met her eyes close-up for the first time. She was definitely a beauty and the lively gray-green eyes seemed to center all her freshness and intrigue.

Self-consciousness suddenly welled up and he thought he might have said too much. After all, she hadn't asked for much beyond social niceties. But she gave him that smile again, which gave his gut a strange twist. He finally located fabric that he knew the Acadian women would put to good use. He also selected a special material of considerable quality with muted flowers for Amalie. The shopkeeper, interested in a sale, was now throwing them fishy looks and was openly resenting the attention the young woman was giving this rustic. But when Rob selected his cloth and paid in hard currency, his mood changed, although there was little doubt that the encounter between these young folk would soon be in the Skenesboro gossip chain. Rob left the shop a little light-headed, and charged down the steps, thinking of little but the gray-green eyes. He missed the bottom one and sprawled on the muddy street into a pile of sodden animal dung, rank with horse piss. He did manage to keep his valuable package out of the slime, but before he could get back on his feet, a number of locals began to guffaw and point at him. At the same time Phoebe emerged with her purchase and joined in the laughter. Rob brushed off what he could and stalked off in a huff, never looking back.

"What the devil happened to you?" Josh queried good-naturedly. But Rob ignored the question and refused to tell Josh anything as the two of them soon rode out of Skenesboro on the Castleton road.

The fine cloth that Rob brought elated the Acadian women and none more than Amalie, who pressed the fabric to her breast and kissed a startled Rob very hard on both cheeks then ran home with her package, laughing all the way. For the moment, Rob forgot his encounter with Phoebe as he felt Amalie's well-sculpted body pressed close. Josh chuckled and slapped his thigh. Even Tomsoc couldn't suppress a smile.

15

The Champlain's shores were blazing with turning leaves as Arnold formed his line of boats behind Valcour Island and set the trap for Carleton. On October 11, the British line sailed past Valcour, not suspecting Arnold's flotilla would appear to their rear. Spotting them near noon, the British turned and formed a battle line lobbing broadsides at the Americans for five hours and inflicting significant damage. But the rebels gave as good as they got and damage to Carleton's flotilla forced the British to withdraw and reform a new battle line. As darkness came on, Arnold knew he had lost too many ships and men and would not win. He chose to run, but preparing to move south meant slipping past the British, which he cleverly did during the night and commenced to make for the protection of the Crown Point batteries. The British were not to be fooled a second time and caught up and captured most of the American fleet two days later. Arnold scuttled or burned his remaining force, then fled on foot to Crown Point. He had goaded Carleton and drawn blood, but the British now had naval control of Champlain. While preparing to attack Crown Point and Ticonderoga, Carleton hesitated and cursed as snow began to fall. He called off the invasion and slowly withdrew his fleet to winter quarters in Canada. Arnold and the impending winter had bought the colonials valuable time, but the rebels knew they'd be back.

Caleb returned to Skenesboro prior to the lake freeze-up, carefully skirting the forts and clusters of colonial militia who were mad as hornets over the loss of their navy and relatives who had died or been maimed by Carleton's victory. The countryside was further polarized and his orders to recruit Tories more agressively made his life more hazardous. None the less, he was confident that there were plenty of disappointed Tories who feared loss of their land and investments. If the rebels had their Minutemen, he surely could rouse at least a regiment for the King.

Despite turbulent times, there was no damper on fall social activities north of Albany. The Skene mansion had regularly hosted the weekend festival over the years that ended the harvest and labor of summer. Country notables of many interests and opinions would appear to drink and dine, cement business deals and step lively with their women at the Harvest Ball. Rebels and Tories shelved politics for a time as business needs and commercial deals trumped differences.

Phoebe Blair and her sister, Jenny, had sown dresses for weeks in preparation and shared the excitement and expectation of meeting men of means, young and old, who might become their interest and support in future life. As a highly eligible bachelor, Caleb was one of these. His interest in the Blair women was no secret.

Caleb's grandfather had early on come north to Albany to associate with the Dutch in the fur trade. He as well as his son had prospered and invested in considerable farmland and forested tracts of land near Lake George. Caleb, while maintaining trading connections with the Mohawks, spent most of his time with agriculture, keenly observing that furs were but a temporary and fleeting commodity compared with the basic food and forest needs of the growing pioneer population. The Elkintons never would have land holdings equaling the scale of the Dutch patroon holders, but they were very comfortable indeed.

A long Indian Summer had preceded the festival and preparations went without a hitch. A small gathering of string musicians from Albany would provide music, assisted by the beautiful Jenny Blair who would perform on the only properly tuned harpsichord north of Albany. Garlands of late fall flowers festooned the walls of Skene's great room which had been cleared for dancing. One would have thought that the rebellion was a continent away as Caleb easily glided over the floor, first with Jenny, then with Phoebe, all the while keeping an ear into the dull roar of background conversation amplified by quantities of liquor.

"I hear that you exchanged pleasantries with a youth from Castleton this summer." Caleb smiled as he danced with Phoebe.

"Yes, he was such a clown, tripping over his own feet as he left Thompson's Dry Goods." She wrinkled her nose describing Rob's misfortune.

"And he was part of Arnold's new navy?"

"No, he said he was a woodsman who helped with the ship building, but was on his way back to Castleton. He had a funny accent." She thought for a moment. "Sounded almost French."

Caleb said nothing, but this information confirmed what he had learned in the street about the Acadians. Getting them to come in with the Tories might be more difficult than he had planned. But he knew of the unrest over in Vermont, the fact that there was no love lost between the Acadians and the southern New England pioneers coming north in a Diaspora. There was even talk that the territory might soon declare itself a separate republic. Rumor had it that Carleton had already sent a secret emissary to talk with the rustic planners about a treaty with Canada.

A clap of hands announced that dancing would cease and that Jenny would sing a solo. Phoebe provided accompaniment on the harpsichord, evidence that the Blair women shared many talents and were not just pretty faces. The Reverend Blair settled on a chair beside the table of food and beamed proudly at his two women. It also became abundantly clear to all that Caleb's interest was now centered on the lovely Jenny. Before the night was over, the two had danced a number of reels and minuets and many eyes rolled as he accompanied her to the carriage, then personally escorted the sisters and the Reverend Blair home.

In mid-January 1777, at a tavern in Windsor, Vermont, a tiny settlement along the Connecticut River, independence was declared and the nation of New Connecticut (later to be called Vermont) arose. The Allens, Ira and Ethan, had a lot to say and, to their credit, the declaration included prescient ideas insisting on the abolition of slavery and indenture contracts, universal male suffrage and public education support. The event did not sit well with the Yorkers or the Continental Congress who viewed this as a loss of territory and a soft spot on the northern frontier. But the pending British invasion would soon muffle both doubts and rustic jubilation.

Carleton had fallen out of favor with the king when it was learned that he had not secured the St. Lawrence Valley or destroyed the invading continental armies of 1775-76. His replacement and reinforcements were in plans percolating in London as Carleton cursed the early winter. General John Burgoyne or "Gentleman Johnny", as he was often called, was the new commander. And despite his ambitions to quietly replace Carleton, "gentleman" he was. He treated his soldiers as a benign lord of the manor might, with a firm hand, yet shunning the aloof manner of many senior officers, often mingling and joking with the ranks, bestowing small, thoughtful favors and encouraging officers to respect their men. This made him popular and helped boost morale. He also liked his creature comforts, pretty women and insisted on traveling with a well-stocked supply of wine and champagne.

The possibilities of a serious blow to northern New England in 1777 were dismissed early on by rebel commanders. After all, hadn't Arnold and Montgomery bloodied the Redcoats in their own backyard? True, no victory was won, but the British lion had a very sore paw indeed, which would take months to heal. King George and his ministers must give ample time to devising a new northern strategy and Howe's pummeling of General Washington on Long Island, New York was surely enough to divert their attention. And Washington's sneak attack on the hapless Hessians at Trenton on Christmas Eve 1776 had clouded hopes of an early British victory.

Despite the colonials having a purloined plan devised by British General Johnny Burgoyne to slice the New England colonies away from the others, such leaked information was not given serious weight. This was a serious miscalculation questioned by some, but only Arnold was vehement in his calls for alarm. His strident demeanor irritated some among Schuyler's staff and won no favor among the leaders ruminating in Philadelphia.

Meeting in private with his friend, Schuyler, he freely vented his feelings. "Philip, we are governed by a pack of sycophants and grafters. How many of those military suck-ups in Philadelphia have even led men in combat?"

"I am of like mind, Benedict, but we both know that men in authority are prone to such pressures."

"Mark my words, the independence of the colonies shall fail if there is not more diligent political and moral integrity shown."

"You are too harsh. Our job is to hold the British at bay while Washington improves his army and bleeds the redcoats into giving up their war. It matters little what the Continental Congress decides at this point."

"Even as they appoint incompetents to lead while lining their pockets with bribes?", Arnold thundered. He immediately softened and added, "You, my friend, are the exception, of course. But while we sit here watching the clouds darken, they do not give a fig for what is happening."

Schuyler merely shook his head and turned to the map lying before him.

Impatient with his superiors and nursing raw feelings about not being given an overdue promotion by a politicized Congress, Arnold soon resigned his commission.

*   *   *

The winter of 1776-77 was harsh. The Acadians hunkered down with their chores of caring for the animals, hauling water and cutting firewood. Josh tutored Rob and Amalie to expand their reading and writing and continued writing his own journal, which he kept under his bed as he did in Boston.

One late afternoon in spring, Rob and Amalie were busy cleaning and repairing the wooden buckets used for the spring sap gathering. It proved to be cold, wet work, made more unpleasant by the sharp breeze blasting off Champlain. Amalie had to blow on her fingers in attempts to warm them.

"Here, let me help." Rob grasped her reddened hands in his and rubbed, but wasn't much help as his, too, were nearly ice cakes. He couldn't help noticing how rough and cracked were her hands, the result of the rough work and life on the farm. His mind wandered and he wondered what Phoebe's hands were like under those fine gloves she wore. "Nothing like these", he ruminated.

Smiling, he suggested that they go to the cowshed and warm their hands on the animals' udders. "Fortunately, they don't mind, having to suffer the hands of the milkers twice daily" With hands pressed between the udder and the inside of the back leg, they soon were rejuvenated. It was warm with animal body heat in the shed and they tarried. Rob decided fetch water for the beasts and asked Amalie to go to the loft and kick down hay for the evening feeding. When she had done so and didn't climb down, he called up to her.

"That's enough. Let's go to supper."

There was no answer so he climbed up to fetch her. She was resting on a woolen blanket covering a hay mound in the corner, watching him through the gloom. When he came near, she laughed and pulled him on top of her. Since time immemorial, nature, without words, communicates the need to replenish the species and, immediately, Rob's lips sought hers and she clasped him hungrily. Despite the chilly drafts from Champlain, most of their clothes came off. There was no guilt. This was animal passion. Both failed to remember Father Henri's long ago admonitions regarding Original Sin. Cooing with pent-up desire, she let his hands roam over her body. Fueled by an overwhelming need that even six yokes of oxen might not stem, his erection found her willing opening and she whimpered once as he plunged full length. His seed poured forth as she clasped him more tightly. As his thrusting became less frequent, she moaned and cried slightly. Thinking he had really hurt her, he rolled away, but still breathed in her ear.

"I'm sorry for the hurt, really am", he blurted

"Oh, don't worry. I'll be fine. It's just a little tear down there. You're like a young bull, Rob, or maybe a little billy goat", she laughed. "Just stay with me for a while." She snuggled into his chest and pulled the rough-woven blanket over them.

As they lay close, skin on skin, basking in the residual warmth of their ardor, he took her hands, again feeling the rough, work-scarred edges. Phoebe swam into his consciousness and he abruptly grew conflicted by what had just happened. In a bit, they dressed, descended and went to supper, Amalie scarcely suppressing her satisfied smile.

16

Rumors now flew thick and fast that the redcoats were coming. Colonial agents verified that thousands of troops, British and German mercenaries, had formed up at St. John and that the new commander, Burgoyne, would lead. The colonial Northern Command acknowledged the earlier warning of this and the rest of the three-pronged battle plan, but dithered. They had no sizeable army to resist and how would they stave off pressure from three directions? A small, sham force of unseasoned militia garrisoned the major bastion of the north, Ticonderoga. The experienced general, Arnold, had already left the area for Philadelphia. Washington was withdrawing into Pennsylvania, flushed with pride at defeating the Hessians, but well aware of his tattered army severely weakened by the debacle on Long Island.

Major Caleb Elkinton had no doubts. His recruiting had not raised the regiment he envisioned, but the two companies of Tories he commanded would do their utmost. Sharp and trim in their forest green uniforms, Tory morale was high knowing they would be the eyes and ears of the Burgoyne's advance. His units now waited out of sight near Fort Ti, making daily sorties to assess its defenses. The softness they found was encouraging. A messenger with this information had already been sent to Burgoyne, who by early June was ready to set sail south.

The weather favored Burgoyne as he sailed down Champlain and prepared to invest Fort Ti. Rumors of invincibility of the combined German-British force and some wild stories about their Mohawk mercenaries created panic on the northern frontier. When English cannon suddenly appeared atop Mt. Defiance virtually looking down on Fort Ti, the rebel General Arthur St. Clair and the defenders made haste in the night of July 4, just a year to the day after the signing of the Declaration of

Independence. They retreated across the lake narrows on top of a chain of boats designed to stop vessels trying to bypass the fort. By some mistake, the destruction of this chain was botched leaving the disengaging rebels nearly as vulnerable as before. A tiny force of provincials was left in the fort to fire cannon randomly as a cover. When Burgoyne's men entered the fort the next day, they found a mere squad of men stone drunk. Fort Ti had fallen without a fight. Temporarily, St. Clair gathered at Fort Independence, on Rattlesnake Hill, an insignificant protuberance across from Fort Ti, not easily defended. But by now his troops were spooked as they continued a confusing retreat down the Castleton Road.

Knowing they had been snookered, the redcoats poured into Vermont in hot pursuit under General Simon Fraser, one of Burgoyne's best. Major Elkinton's Tories who knew the territory well were the lead unit comprising the very point of this British spear. Ian MacKensie called his little hamlet of farmers together and urged them to drive their livestock into the woods to a hastily constructed enclosure away from the thoroughfare. He knew what soldiers, especially hungry ones, would do to replenish their stores while on the march. And it wasn't just redcoats that were a worry. Sharp-eyed Yorker land speculators and colonists from over the Green Mountains regularly coveted the prosperity of the Acadians. And still painfully fresh in mind was the knowledge that New England colonists, eager for Acadian lands, had fomented the great French Diaspora of 1755 from Grande Pre. *Le Grande derangement.*

17

The evening of July 6 had been hot and sultry. Over Champlain and the forts, thunderstorms had crashed, rolling ominously south. Ian and the Acadians watched as scores of exhausted troops, many wild-eyed with fear, slogged past the inn. After drinking from the well, both officers and men told tales of the superior army about to overtake them. St. Clair, recognizing his vulnerability, formed a rear guard to delay the British, make them deploy and give the rest of his army a chance to make safe their retreat. Colonel Seth Warner would command this array of troops with the assistance of Continentals from Massachusetts and New Hampshire under Colonels Francis and Hale.

Elkinton's Tory scouts found Warner's defenses on Monument Hill very early on July 7. No shots were fired as Caleb reported back to Fraser. Less than a mile away was a rock outcrop called Mount Zion which afforded an excellent view of Warner's line. Caleb positioned himself there with a spyglass to provide updates to Fraser on what the rebels were doing.

The first of Burgoyne's redcoats to come down the road to the inn at dawn were light infantry. Ian scowled as the first British he'd seen in nearly a decade marched up in disciplined ranks. The Acadians trooped out excitedly to see them, initially impressed with their fine scarlet coats and white breeches. Their commander halted them by the inn, remained mounted and queried Ian.

"You do speak English, sir?"

"Aye", Ian replied guardedly.

"Your village consists of Acadian French, I am told. Do you swear allegiance to the King or the rebels we pursue?"

"We do not raise our hand against or patronize any group and seek only to nourish our own and aid those in need."

The officer grew red-faced. "My scouts tell me that rebels passing here just hours ago took food and water."

"Yes", Ian agreed calmly." "And your men may do the same. It is needed by all in this weather."

"Where are your cattle and meat animals."

"They are dispersed for safety, sir." Ian met the mounted man eyeball to eyeball.

"I'll bet they are, probably running away with the rebels." He pointed his sword toward the Castleton Road.

"No, I assure you they are not."

The officer turned and told his sergeants to have the men scour the outbuildings. They soon returned having found nothing. Turning once again to Ian, he shouted, "You had better be telling the truth, old man, because if not, Burgoyne will lay waste to all of you."

"March on", he commanded the troops.

A mile away from the Castelton military road in a copse of hemlock, Rob and Josh and a small group of Acadian men and women sweated as they completed a makeshift wooden enclosure. They had chosen carefully so that part of the pen provided access to a small brook for water for the animals. No air moved in the copse and legions of mosquitos took a blood breakfast from both humans and beasts. Rising like a plague from the brook were blackflies seeking their share of mammalian gore. Nothing to do now but wait, hoping the armies would press on south via the road and leave them alone. It wasn't long before the British light infantry stumbled onto rebel skirmishers waiting by a curve in the road. The animal keepers dreaded the popping of the muskets nearby, but knew their best response was to keep the beasts calm and lie low.

More British joined the infantry and the Continentals backed off, having drawn first blood. Redcoats on their tail, they ran for cover up Monument Hill where the main brushy tangle breastworks commanded by Colonel Francis had been constructed.

The redcoats hesitated for a time before attempting to cross the brook upstream from the hidden Acadians. A fusillade of withering fire killed their commanding officer and a score of others. Regrouping, the British drove back the few defenders, splashed across the brook and advanced on Monument Hill, but were repulsed by more deadly musketry from Francis's Continentals behind the breastworks. Twice they tried and failed. Caleb watched all this with consternation, fully appreciating the skill of the rebel rear guard. Spotting a chink in the eastern portion of the breastwork, he immediately sent this information to Fraser. In the ensuing lull, Caleb could see that the Continentals, too, were taking casualties. If Fraser moved quickly to flank their position, they could be bested.

The Acadians at the animal enclosure could hear the fray, but could not conclude who were winning and where the next strike would be. The cattle and sheep remained quiet, but Rob noticed that when they went to drink at the brook, they would throw their heads up and shake them from side to side, refusing to take water. Investigating, he found that the stream coming from the battle area was turning red, staining his cupped hands, leaving him with a sickened feeling. He'd seen animal slaughter, but never dreamed how this much blood might be lost in a pitched battle. Amalie noticed his pallor and pushed several animals aside to urge him out of the water and onto the small hummock of hemlock boughs where the others were resting.

The sudden silence made them all nervous. Tomsoc emerged from out of nowhere and whispered in Josh's ear that Mohawks were coming near. Within minutes, a green-clad white man in brown leggings stood in front of them, leader of a dozen Mohawks, painted for a fight. Seeing that the Acadians had no weapons, Caleb urged them to stay put and tend their livestock. "Venture to the battle will cause you grave danger." His savage band fingered their scalping knives suggestively. Like a dream, the Tory and his band then glided noiselessly into the forest making for Monument Hill. Within minutes, the sound of singing on the Castelton Road began. The Acadians quaked at the unfamiliar sound in a strange language until Josh held up his hand and urged quiet. These were the Brunswickers, Burgoyne's German mercenaries. Fraser had rightly concluded that to pound away frontally was folly. A flanking movement would sweep the Continentals out of their fortified line and open the road to the main rebel force. Sheer numbers were against Colonel Francis and the defenders as they tried to disengage seeking shelter behind the next ridge. It soon became a rout, causing the rebels to leave their dead and wounded strewn across the battlefield.

Caleb and his Mohawks crested Monument Hill first with the fire-breathing light infantry right behind. Spotting the wounded Continentals, the Redcoats howled in anger, having lost many comrades, and commenced to run at the wounded, bayonets to the fore. Caleb ordered them to stop, but none would listen until he pulled out his pistol and thrust it in the face of the nearest redcoat. "Touch these men and you die!", he shouted and struck the man a hard blow to the head. The man collapsed, but soon was up with his musket ranged on Caleb. "You're just like these damned rebels. We'll have them as we want them, by God!" A shot rang out and the man collapsed again, clutching his forearm. An officer on horseback charged across the field and threatened to run down any redcoat who refused to drop his musket.

Returning to Caleb, he told him to put the pistol away. "There will be no slaughter of the enemy this day."

Only then did Caleb recognize the rider as General Fraser himself. The dozen Mohawks stood skulking by the brush line, again fingering their scalping knives. Caleb told them to put the knives away and help lift wounded redcoats into the farm wagons transporting them back to the care of military surgeons. He could hear intermittent musket fire on the ridge to the south, but the battle was over. It was scarcely mid-morning. The rebels were on the run, but they had stopped Burgoyne and saved most of St. Clair's main army to fight another day.

Rob, noting the reduction of gunfire and cheering of the Brunswickers flanking the rebels, told Josh and Tomsoc to stay with the tenders of the livestock while he went to see if it were safe to return to Ian and the settlement. "No, don't go there!", cried Amalie, clinging to his sleeve, clearly recalling the warning from the Tory officer. But he shook her off and was soon out of sight slogging up the brook.

As the noise of battle dwindled away, the Acadians resigned themselves to wait in the hemlock copse. Noon came and went. There was no food available, as their hurried departure with the animals from the settlement had left no time for preparation. By mid-afternoon just when patience was thin and tempers grew short, Tomsoc held up his hand for silence. Coming through the brush on the far side of the brook was a squad of soldiers, green-backed Tories, and a band of men in peasant clothing. They entered the enclosure looking covetously at the animals. The Acadians silently stood their ground while the Tory sargeant explained that these were teamsters with him and demanded that the animals be returned to the settlement. No one moved, but emerging suddenly from the brush was the peasant leader, a mammoth person with discolored front teeth who glared at them, then, smiling, caught sight of Josh and whistled.

"I'll be damned, if it ain't little Dogshit!"

Rob reached the Castelton Road just as some farm wagons from the settlement passed with loads of redcoat wounded. Some moaned and cried out as the carts lumbered over ruts and bumps. Others were ominously still and Rob paused, shocked at their condition. Continental prisoners marched alongside this wretched cargo, assuring that the wounded did not fall off. A small guard of redcoats plodded behind to keep everyone in line.

"You, there", an officer cried angrily, "Get in line with your fellow prisoners."

Rob came quickly out of his stupor and joined the caravan, knowing that to do otherwise was to invite a musket ball. He knew the twists and turns of the road and was sure that at the right moment he would be able to slip away into the woods. But the officer kept a sharp eye on them and soon they reached the settlement. The inn had been turned into a makeshift hospital where army surgeons were triaging the wounded. The growing pile of motionless bodies and severed arms and legs was frightful. Terror was clearly evident on the faces of the Acadians being pressed into care giving. Ian caught sight of Rob and rushed to his side only to be butted away by a guard's musket. Rob made sure that his father knew he was unhurt as he was led away to one of the cowsheds where rebel prisoners were accumulating.

Caleb watched this sorry scene impatiently. While the British officers were euphoric in victory, he knew that the rebels were not to be underestimated. And there were still many dead and wounded to be gathered up on Monument Hill. "Prepare to return for more wounded as soon as those wagons are available", he ordered one of his ensigns. "And take with you those healthy prisoners to help find and load quickly. Time is running out for our soldiers to get help from these surgeons."

General Fraser had other problems. To pursue the defeated further into the country would invite guerilla attacks on his lengthened supply line. And Burgoyne had told him not to widen the gap with the main army waiting at Fort Ti. At least for the present, Gentleman Johnny was keeping his eye on the main objective of splitting New England off from the rest of the colonies.

Rob huddled with the others in pools of blood on the wagon bed, chafing at his decision to leave the livestock enclosure. His dejection deepened when coming up the road was the Acadians' hoofed treasure and his friends all under Tory guard. He caught Josh's eye as they passed, then saw Justice grinning malevolently. "Guess what we got, boys?", he announced to all in a loud voice. "Enough meat to take us to Albany and a couple of morsels for dessert." He chuckled and nodded towards Amalie and the Acadian women. Rob rose up to confront the giant, but was knocked flat in the slippery blood by a Tory musket butt. By the time he recovered, the wagons were far along and nothing could be gained by more confrontation, so he sat in the blood and rubbed his throbbing shoulder. The ensign commanded more speed as up ahead everyone heard the wounded crying for help. They loaded broken bodies as fast as compassion would allow, but when Rob moved to tend wounded Continentals, he was prodded at musket point move on. Refusing the order, he became surrounded by other Tories who sneered at both Rob and the wounded.

"How can you deny these men the same treatment as your redcoats?", he yelled angrily. Just when tempers seemed to boil over, Caleb rode onto the scene. "What 's the trouble here?" he demanded. Rob recognized him at once as the leader of the Mohawks at the livestock enclosure. "Merciful God", cried Rob. "Your soldiers have no pity for their countrymen!"

"This youth is a stubborn rebel, just like these vermin lying here", snarled one of the Tories.

Caleb and Rob stared at each other for a time, then Caleb dismounted and told the men to gather as many wounded rebels as they could find for the return trip to the inn. Standing close to Rob, he held his eye.

"You are Acadian, no doubt?"

"Yes, sir." he responded proudly.

"Why are you among these prisoners?"

"I was taken on the road by your men as I was returning to the settlement."

"And were you armed at the time?"

"No, sir."

"Then come with me." Caleb led him across the field to a dead man lying in the grass. Standing over the body was a senior officer in conference with Von Riedesel, the Brunswick commander. Rob remained silent and aloof until General Fraser pointed at the body and, turning to Rob, asked, "Do you know this person?" Rob looked down at the lifeless form. Indeed he had seen him pass the inn during the rebel retreat, but only recognized him as their leader.

"He is the Colonel who commanded the Massachusetts Continentals as they passed yesterday."

"Ah, so we do have the brilliant Colonel Ebenezer Francis here", sighed Fraser. "An able commander, according to you, Von Riedesel. As you suggest, we shall bury him on this spot with full military honors in the morning." He turned to Rob." Thank you, young man. I gather from your speech, you are of the Acadian settlement?" Rob nodded, then, thrusting out his lower lip, made a request.

"Sir, your teamsters have collected our farm animals to slaughter and supply your army. They are our only means of survival and would wish that they be returned to us."

The officers caught their breath sharply at this impudence, but Fraser smiled magnanimously as a proper victor should. "It shall be done", he assured Rob.

Fraser and his officers rode off, returning to the inn and the wounded. Rob and the other prisoners finished loading redcoat and homespun-clad casualties, living and dead, onto the carts and prepared for departure. Dead Continentals still lay on the field, but Caleb promised that local farmers would be paid to complete their burials by the next day. As the wagons bumped on up the road, Caleb ordered Rob to remain. Suspiciously eyeing the Tory major, he jumped on the last wagon, but was immediately dragged off and clasped by two of Caleb's men. He struggled and shot them all dark looks to no avail.

"You'll stay with me a while. I need someone who knows the Abenaki and French tongues. You will be well-treated, but don't try to escape if you value your life."

Seething with contempt, he was bound and seated on a horse, then tethered to and led away by Caleb's mount. Caleb ignored his protests as the Tory band cut back north on an obscure track away from the road and the settlement.

Josh and Amalie dutifully returned their livestock to the sheds. He couldn't believe that Justice had found him and his urge was to get away fast rather than risk being returned to the Bartons. But a little thinking told him that Justice couldn't be among the British for the petty reason of jumped indenture.

But how did the bastard get here? He must have departed Boston with Gage, then somehow joined this campaign. He would never make it as a soldier. They must have other jobs for him to do. A teamster-Ha!

Just then Fraser and his staff rode up and asked to speak to Ian. Josh and Amalie couldn't hear the discussion, but almost immediately, the teamsters hovering around the cattle pens like hungry wolves were dispersed. Justice put on an angry face and started up the road with the departing troops. He noticed Josh's smile and shook his fist, but kept going. Fraser had made good on his promise, but Josh knew they had not seen the last of Justice.

After burying his dead, Fraser pulled his force back to Fort Ti later the next day taking prisoners and wounded with him. Except for the few remaining terrifying memories, the settlement returned to normal. By the end of the week, the rebel dead had been buried, as many wounded had been cared for by the Acadians as possible and stragglers and deserters shown the way north or south. This did nothing to allay the worry of Ian, Josh and Amalie when Rob could not be accounted for.

18

Rob, with Caleb in the lead, continued north, skirting the traveled road and soon came to Champlain, Fort Ti looming across the narrows. Burgoyne's army tents lay spread out on the flats near the walls, supply and transport ships anchored near the rebel's defensive boom of boats, now rapidly being dismantled by his engineers. Rob was impressed, having never seen an army of this size, nearly 9500 men, mostly British regulars, but with many Hessians and some Tories and Mohawks. The numbers of Tory recruits were swelling, but, with few exceptions such as Caleb's unit, were assigned to support rather than combat duty. British pride in their own may have been the reason. Burgoyne, not colonial Tory irregulars, was going to bask in the glory of this battlefield. Curiously, the composition of troops was ill suited to the campaign. Hessian cavalry were dismounted with no horses to ride. Many cannon were being off-loaded from the ships and what horses there were harnessed to their caissons. The roads south over, which the campaign would travel, were primitive and Burgoyne would soon find out that rebel woodsmen would make them nearly impassable. Horse-drawn wagons were in short supply, yet these were the most critical conveyances on which army supply would have to depend as they extended their march south. Burgoyne, alone, used many wagons and carts for his personal belongings including wine, champagne and a full tea service. Other wagons carried the women's finery of officers' wives who accompanied the caravan and for Burgoyne's alleged mistress. This army also harbored hundreds of camp followers, many of them women who attended the army in various capacities, including prostitution. Rob rightly concluded that the primary role of that scummy reprobate, Justice, was to keep this mobile brothel intact, not serve as teamster.

As they entered the fort's main gate, Rob caught the ebullient spirit of the place. Spirits were high with enthusiasm that this campaign was to be easy and short. Troops paraded smartly across the reviewing area while a phalanx of officers welcomed Fraser's returning redcoats and the Brunswickers from the recent rout of the colonials. Even the walking wounded were all smiles as they received these accolades. Only the small clusters of rebel prisoners walked with eyes downcast to a holding area under the canvass overhang near the outer walls. Caleb and Rob passed the watchful eye of Burgoyne himself who acknowledged Caleb's salute and appeared quite full of himself over this first engagement.

Caleb assigned Rob to the control of an artillery battery as an auxiliary to assist them where needed. The cannoneers regarded him as a servant, but quickly recognized his skill with their horses and, while keeping a watchful eye, left him alone. Afternoon was fading and delicious odors began emanating from the cooking pots. This army was well fed and provisioned and he suddenly was very hungry.

Jeremy Van Orton had fallen in one of the first withering rebel volleys. His unit continued up Monument Hill, leaving him bleeding in the forest. He'd tried to stanch the flow and had crawled deeper into the woods where it was cooler, knowing that he would be sought after and rescued. But no one came, despite his calling and he soon swooned from blood loss. It was dark when he returned to his senses. His wounds had ceased oozing, but still no searchers came and he knew that survival meant getting food and water soon.

Amalie went about her chores, feeding the cattle and shooing the sheep into their pens for safety against nocturnal predators. Counting up, she noticed that a newborn was missing. Night was falling, but she retraced her steps up to the hillside pasture and finding nothing, combed the forest edge. Rounding a huge boulder, she gasped in horror. A Brown Bess musket was aimed at her bosom, but what made chills run through her was not the bright red coat, but the coal-black face which topped it. Nestled in one arm of this soldier was the young sheep, but this first sight of a black man left her mute. He spoke first in a tongue she barely grasped, but came to her senses, realizing that the man was wounded and had been missed or purposely left for dead by his comrades. He must have crawled some distance as his trousers were muddied and torn. Dried bloodstains, a flecked brown, sullied the lower part of his tunic. He lowered the musket and pointed to his wounds. She fought off the cold fear urge to dash away and, in shaking voice, told him to release the lamb and she would bring help. He lay back as she backed away around the stone and double-timed it back to the settlement. Josh would know what to do next.

By the time Josh and several Acadians got to the pasture, the black soldier was unconscious. They relieved him of his Brown Bess and loaded him onto a litter. Josh noted that blowflies were already crawling over him searching for his wounds in which to lay their eggs. A black face in the community roused much excitement as few had ever seen an African before, not to mention one in a redcoat. But they tended him like the other wounded. A musket ball had gone through his upper leg, but despite debilitating pain and blood loss, had hit nothing vital and lodged just under the skin of his upper rump. Aided by Amalie, Josh slit open the skin and removed the ball, then sutured the wound as best he could in the fashion he had observed done by the British surgeons. Another ball had taken away some of his left breast, laying muscle tissue bare. It was here that the flies sought a maternity ward for their eggs. The soldier lay limp for days, but gradually improved as fluids were administered and broth was consumed. Josh kept the wounds clean with frequent change of bandages and careful removal of maggots hatched from the eggs, allowing only several healthy specimens to remain for clearing up necrotic tissue. His intuition told him to remove them all, but a British surgeon he had assisted, had let the maggots feed, and this had shown to be an important shield against life-threatening gangrene.

"What do they call you?" Josh had seen blacks in Boston and had learned the names of several who came to the shop to pick up wares. He was always surprised by names that were often those given by English masters.

"I be Jeremy Van Orton, a soldier for King George."

Josh learned that the man had been promised his freedom if he served with the British. As the slave of a landowner in Albany, he aspired to be one of the freedmen class of blacks who had nearly the same rights and legal standing as whites and who owned property and goods. Josh immediately understood his plight and urged him to call his commander on the promise made, as he likely would always be lame and not fit for further duty as a lobsterback. He assured that the man would return to the garrison at Fort Ti and two weeks later put the wounded black on a farm cart and drove him north to the British.

19

Burgoyne's euphoria knew no bounds. So confident was he that the rebels were on the run that he decided to float his men and vessels directly down to the end of Champlain. The less attractive alternative was to take his vessels apart and carry them overland to Lake George where they would have to be put back together for the voyage to Fort George. On his crude map, linear distances seemed somewhat comparable if not insignificant. A straight shot south to Skenesboro was more direct, even if it meant more overland march from there to the Hudson River. The majority of his supplies would catch up more slowly and be floated via Lake George to Fort George as planned. From there to Fort Anne it was a short ten miles to where the main army would soon be. His Tory spies told him that the two forts to the south, Edward and Miller, were mere cowsheds and the prize, Albany, lay immediately beyond.

It all seemed simple enough. Never mind that the narrow and tortuous waters of lower Champlain made ships and troop scows vulnerable to attack from shore artillery. His spies had also told him that there was little concern as the rebels had no guns of any size and were falling all over each other in front of his red tide. Besides, he had been invited by Captain Skene to tarry in his village where a decent mansion awaited him. To assure this, he'd even sent a force south as the rebels were being chased at Hubbardton. This resulted in a sharp firefight near the village that broke the rebel hold and allowed the capture of several cannon and supplies. So with no further delay, he left a garrison holding Fort Ti and sailed south. He would stay at the Skenes mansion until his supplies at Fort George were secure.

Despite its small size and frontier ambiance, Skenesboro at the lower tip of Lake Champlain represented the northernmost piece of New York civilization above Albany. It had prospered with trade as the beginning of the direct water route to Canada. Burgoyne noted that it was but a dozen miles from Fort Anne to which the defeated rebels had retreated. With ease that fort could easily be secured and used as a base should the rebels regain their courage. As more troops disembarked and set up camp in the surrounding farmland, Burgoyne moved in with Skene, lock, stock and barrel, having found just what he wanted.

The British presence in Skenesboro rallied Hudson Valley Tory sentiments. Loyalist recruitments improved and civilians cheered Burgoyne's arrival. The Reverend Blair and family attended as a regiment of redcoats marched through town on their way to a bivouac area. Caleb with Rob in tow arrived after dark and went straight to the Elkinton homestead. Waiting there was the Blair family. Both of the young women embraced Caleb as he came through the door. Rob, now unshackled, remained on the porch until acknowledged by Caleb. The sight of Phoebe and the Blair family association with the Tory leader gave him a start, but he concealed his confusion. She recognized him immediately and threw him a slight smile. Caleb made the proper introductions.

"This is Rob MacKensie who accompanies me as interpreter. He is of the Acadian settlement in Hubbardton and prefers to remain a non-combatant. The Reverend eyed Rob sharply and spoke first.

"You're the chap who assisted us last year near Fort Anne, if I'm not mistaken. Your role then appeared to be helping transit the rebel artillery."

Rob remained silent, never shrinking from the stern looks.

"Nevertheless", the clergyman continued as he extended a hand, "your help in our time of need was most generous."

Caleb completed the introductions and gave Rob his leave to take care of the horses. He was tormented, never dreaming that Phoebe would be here re-entering his life so soon again. The temptation was great to mount and make haste to the Castleton Road and home, but that was too risky within an army of lobsterbacks. Besides, Phoebe's connection to Caleb was a new twist that he had to learn more about.

Back at Fort Ti, Colonel Charles Penfield, Burgoyne's supply chief, had to goad his staff preparing the transfer of materials over the three and a half-mile portage to Lake George. An insufficient number of scows meant additional on-site construction, but the relative ease of the invasion had sapped the army's diligence. Besides, Burgoyne's devil-may-care pause in Skenesboro suggested that time was not really important. Penfield did not share this confidence, yet his job remained giving the army the support it needed. "Those damn camp followers are no asset to our mission," he grumbled to himself. "Especially that blackguard, Justice". He had come to distrust this teamster as completely unreliable. Fortunately, the slow progress of the army had made Penfield's job easier. The supply lines were still relatively short and if he could stockpile at Fort George, the generals would have easier access for the final thrust to Albany. Success, however, depended on continued protection against the small bands of guerillas poking at his wagon trains and the limited food and forage carried by the army. Time was clearly not on the side of the British. If they did not take Albany with its reputed vast supply depot by late summer, Penfield would have precious little for his teamsters to move. He'd already sent teams out to scour the countryside for provisions, but the rebels had hidden or driven off everything of value. Even the Tories were pleading poor.

"Ah, Major Skene, your accommodations are just fine." Burgoyne was well pleased to be at the head of Champlain, within, he judged, a "stone's throw" of Albany. Skene's promotion was but a small token of the commander's generosity.

"My honor to have you here, sir." Skene was not just being cordial. The British and Hessians had swept the rebel scum out of his village and lands. Their brief occupation had raised havoc, but he knew his holdings were now secure. Any damages could easily be repaired and his businesses would again flourish.

Casting his eye around Skene's great room, Burgoyne saw possibilities and turning to General Von Riedesel, asked "Could your musicians fit here and provide us with a bit of entertainment?" Riedesel, caught off guard, hesitated, then quickly affirmed. "Yes, my friend, what do you have in mind?"

"We all need some relief, some culture in this rustic land. No offense to you and your generosity, Skene," he quickly added. Then to all assembled he announced, "My play, *Maid of the Oaks*, humble though it is, will have its premiere North American performance in your mansion. The esteemed Garrick can't be here to help us, but we'll fill the cast with some of my talented officers and a few of the lovely lasses who are with us. Your Brunswickers are skilled musicians and can provide us a bit of Telemann's Tafelmusik during dinner and later some Bach, father and son, even perhaps a work of that child, Mozart. You Teutons are not only brave warriors, but have been the talk of Britain ever since old Handel brought his melodies to London years ago." Riedesal and Skene exchanged glances, but nodded gracefully.

Gentleman Johnny was ecstatic. His casting for *Maid of theOaks* was now complete with Colonel Penfield's wife, a frequent visitor to Skenes's mansion, in the main heroine's role. A pity, the Colonel had remained at Fort Ti. As rehearsals progressed, Burgoyne opened his supply of wine and champagne to the troupe and the Skenesboro episode turned into a pleasant celebration. So magnanimous became the commander that the entire army was to receive an extra ration of rum on the evening of the performance. Colonel Penfield, already worrying over the supply train, was directed to give Burgoyne's personal wagons top priority for Skenesboro delivery.

Colonel Penfield's wife, Lady Charlotte, was a dark haired beauty seen often in Burgoyne's company. A lively personality and blessed with a quick wit, she was his first choice and easily fulfilled the role of heroine in the play. Rehearsals commenced immediately and her regular attendance at the mansion afforded the Blair women easy access to this woman who gave them generously of her time. Both Jenny and Phoebe delighted learning about the goings-on of society in the mother country. A few tongues wagged at Lady Penfield's presence as Burgoyne's favorite, but she made sure that the Blair women stayed at the mansion and served as her buffer against any unwanted attention by the commander. It was she who suggested that the Blair women should add their musical talents to the planned program. Burgoyne agreed and even had a small spinet piano unloaded from his personal train so the sisters could perfect their songs.

It was during practice that Rob first heard Phoebe's rendition of Handel's music. His untutored, yet sensitive ear had heard no such music before, his upbringing limited to rustic Acadian dances with fiddle and the clatter of sticks and clog dancing to keep time. As he tended Caleb's mounts outside the mansion, he was now easily distracted. Each day there were redcoats and Hessian blue marching to and fro to the gruff commands of the sergeants. He regularly observed Gentleman Johnny himself mixing easily with his troops, officers, sergeants and privates alike. With none of the haughty distancing so prevalent in the officer class, no wonder that the men of the Royal Army held him in esteem.

Caleb regularly joined in the war councils in the great room. Having Jenny nearby practicing on the spinet or the harpsichord made his visits that much more pleasant and he would often remain after the meetings to walk through the gardens with her. Rob stayed with the horses, but would catch sight of Phoebe departing for the Elkinton homestead. After several days and brief smiles, she stopped to chat and soon he forgot about the animals after carefully securing them outside the mansion and accompanied her the mile and a half home. In fact, he was quickly forgetting much about his former life at the settlement.

20

Josh, Tomsoc and the Redcoat went north on the military road, headed for Fort Ti. Still recovering, the black soldier lay on the farm wagon bed, wincing when sharply jolted in the rutted road. Rounding a bend, they passed through a series of rocky crags, overhung by tall trees and fissured deeply enough to conceal large predators. The easily impressionable Acadians feared "the notch" with good reason as it was the sad place where Father Henri was slain. Further, a catamount had once made a lightning strike and killed two nanny goats before carrying another one off, reinforcing their fears. Since then they had most carefully tended the passage of their livestock here on the way to sales at the forts. Broad daylight now made contact with any big cats very unlikely, but, sensing trouble, Tomsoc became alert and urged Josh to make speed. Suddenly, a dozen riders in peasant dress slipped out of the crags and cut them off, ahead and behind. Josh recognized at once some of the same teamsters who had attempted to rustle the Acadian livestock. A horseman came alongside the wagon from behind and looked down at Josh.

"Seems you and me keep meeting up, Dogshit." Justice smiled triumphantly as he grasped the bridle of Josh's horse. "You and that neggar on your way to Fort Ti? Maybe a little ransom money for turning him in? Well, we can give some escort. Your Injun friend can find his way back to the Frenchies by himself."

Tomsoc eyed the musket behind his seat, but one of Justice's cronies already had the drop on him with an ugly looking pistol. Another rider dismounted and scooped up the musket. Justice motioned for Tomsoc to get moving. In one swift movement, he was off the wagon and into the forest, surprising all of them. One rider raised his musket for a parting shot, but Justice shouted him to lay off.

"We got more booty here than we came for" he chuckled as he tied the wagon's reins to his saddle.

Three hours later they passed through Fort Ti's main gate. Colonel Penfield watched as they came by the officer's quarters. "What have you there, Justice?" He inquired quite scornfully, knowing full well that there must be something ignoble afoot.

"Captured this Frenchie making off with one of our wounded, sir." He spat out the falsehood with sly obsequious acknowledgement of the major's rank.

"See that you get that wounded man to the surgeon and bring the young lad to me."

Justice scowled, but recovered and adopted an obsequious tone. "This one's slippery, sir. May I suggest that he be put in with the other rebel prisoners?"

Penfield hesitated, then recalled that the fort garrison commander was expecting him. He had little time for this interruption and even less time for this scoundrel.

"So be it." He turned and made for the headquarters. Justice smirked, turned Jeremy over to the medical orderly and marched Josh off to the fort goal.

The prison was overcrowded and stank to high heaven. Rebels had had their wounds cared for, but not given any space for recovery. Josh was yet another unwanted body in the teeming hole, a dug cavern in the lowest part of the fort. Most prisoners were lounging on the dirt floor, still wet from seepage and recent rain runoff. A few domineering ones had staked out wall space where they could at least lean against the support logs and keep all but the feet dry. In a far corner on some raised pallets lay the wounded, their torn flesh the source of the sickening stench exacerbated by the summer heat and closeness of the goal. Josh squeezed his way to a tiny chink of light amid groans of protest from the men. Many of them were shrugging and scratching, a behavior he knew meant the presence of body lice. Under these conditions it would be only hours before newcomers would be infested. On some of the pallets, carefully avoided by other prisoners, lay unmoving men, their bodies covered with ruptured pustules which added a peculiar, yet familiar odor. Smallpox. Josh wracked his brain for answers, knowing full well he had only a short time to escape this place.

Next morning, Jeremy was reunited with his comrades when several other of King George's blacks visited him in the hospital. But Jeremy wasted no time with their sympathy.

"There be a young man in the goal who saved me and you have to get him away."

"That not easy, Jeremy", said a giant comrade with corporal rank.

"But he can't stay here. That teamster who wants to collect a ransom kidnapped him as he was helping me reach here. He escaped from a master worse than what you and I know and deserves freedom." He searched their faces for support. "That boy and his people saved my life."

The corporal rolled his eyes. "For you, Jeremy, we'll try." He motioned for his pals to join him outside where they concocted a plan.

"Joshua Shattuck, come out." The goal sentry cracked open the goal's door and held his nose. Josh pushed his way to the guard who whacked him on the shoulder and thrust him into the arms of three black redcoats. "These men will escort you to headquarters."

But with all the coming and going on the parade ground, no one noticed when the escort slipped out the gate with their charge. Marching in formation with arms drawn and the big corporal in the lead, no one dared challenge them as they made their way across the remains of the floating boom and foot bridge to Fort Independence. On reaching dry land, the corporal flashed a grin and told Josh to keep walking. "You don't know who got you out of the hellhole and you never seen us, O.K.? But Jeremy, he now smiling again."

Josh nodded and kept going down the military road, soon to put the British army behind him.

Justice was furious, but no bluster about his prisoner's escape could move Colonel Penfield. His orders were to deliver another three of Burgoyne's personal supply wagons overland to Skenesboro immediately. He would accompany the caravan and Justice would drive the lead wagon. This made sense as the flotilla with the main supplies wouldn't be ready to shove off down Lake George until the next week and he must be ready to direct the landing at Fort George. Moreover, he had been too long away from Lady Charlotte.

The ox-drawn wagons and small redcoat guard contingent made slow progress over the rough track alongside Lake Champlain and required a stop for the night in dense woods a dozen miles short of Skenesboro. Sentries had yet to be posted when colonial guerillas attacked. The teamsters melted into the woods, letting the lobsterbacks face a withering volley from hidden rebels. Penfield quickly realized they were vulnerable and hoisted a white flag just as a musket ball whizzed through his tunic and breeches, taking away a sizeable piece of his rump. In minutes the rebels had rounded up and disarmed the hapless troops, less a young ensign who had escaped by mounting the colonel's horse and galloping off towards Skenesboro. The rebel leader, euphoric in his luck at bagging a high-ranking officer for ransom, did his best to comfort the wounded colonel and construct a litter in one of the wagons.

Justice, ever the chameleon, emerged from hiding and welcomed his captors. Breaking out a quantity of Burgoyne's champagne, he soon became more rebel ally than captive. The rebels reversed the caravan and immediately set out east for the Green Mountains knowing that the escaped ensign would have redcoats back here at first light. Ever the renegade, Justice plied the rebel leader with Burgoyne's champagne, coaxing out valuable bits of information on rebel strength and maneuvers, knowing that this just may come in handy when he was done with his captors.

An exhausted horse and rider clattered down Skenesboro's thoroughfare and halted at the mansion. Guards stopped the young officer at the door despite his protests and imperative demand to see Burgoyne's aide-de-camp at once.

"The General says not to disturb while the play is in progress. Just wait outside and someone will see you later." This from a captain of Royal Marines who was giving the ensign a caustic look. Deflated, the young officer retired to the nearby tavern for food and drink, having not eaten since breakfast.

21

The evening of the performance was perfect. A cool, fir-scented breeze swept in from the Adirondacks and a clear, star-filled sky vaulted over the encampment. Burgoyne's officers and their wives paraded into Skene's mansion, assisted by servants and non-commissioned officers, playing their roles to perfection. The evening's entertainment included the play, plus musical renditions by the Brunswickers as well as songs by the Blair sisters. Caleb insisted that Rob don some of his own civilian garb and come along while he became resplendent in his green Tory uniform. Rob had initially balked, but became genuinely curious when he learned that Phoebe would be there.

"Maid of the Oaks", was most entertaining, the amateur actors showing surprising skill and finesse. This had been preceeded by several Handel pieces performed by the Blair women. Dancing followed, the Brunswickers adeptly performing waltzes and reels. Rob was standing on the rear portico, hearing the music and watching through open doors, as Phoebe gracefully stepped and clasped hands with young officers. The beauty and talent of the dancers mesmerized him as it did many of the audience. Nothing like it had ever been seen or heard at the settlement. The Brunswickers deftly coaxed a series of minuets from their instruments. Rob could envision the lithe hands of Phoebe caressing those same sweet sounds out of the spinet. Hands nothing like those of Amalie, work-roughened and scarred. He remembered vividly the days of hard work and boredom of farm life and vowed not to return to a life without friends in clean, colorful clothes and women in starched dresses. The sweet odor of flowers in this garden certainly trumped the sour smells of the settlement. Caleb had caused him to shed his rustic clothing, providing tailored garments of his own. Further, Rob was coming to respect this Tory officer who, although his captor, had impressed him with the fairness and care shown to his men.

Applause and laughter roused him from his thoughts and told him that the dancing had ended. The partygoers implored the Blairs to continue with more music and a Handel aria from *Theodora* soon drifted out into the soft summer air. "Angels ever bright and fair, take me to your care." He knew who it was by the elegant voice and became enthralled, thinking only of how he and the singer might soon be alone together in this garden.

As the singing ended, Rob was nearly bowled over by the grimy ensign desperately seeking access to a Burgoyne aide. Accepted finally, like a skunk at a garden party, he poured out his news to a startled captain who swiftly retired with two senior officers to an adjacent room. Forthwith, the captain returned and slithered up to Burgoyne and Lady Charlotte who sat smiling to more Brunswicker music. His face became clouded and he nodded decisively to what the captain was sharing. Lady Charlotte's color drained and she rose, giving her nearby maidservant a weak smile. Moving swiftly to a deserted anteroom, she broke into quiet sobs. Jenny Blair had followed her exit and now wrapped her arms over the shaking shoulders.

The players and merrymakers streamed out of the Skene mansion to continue to party on the lawn. Rob thought their comings and goings to be like moths and fireflies as their shadowy outlines flitted by candlelight streaming from the mansion's windows. He caught sight of Phoebe and moved to her side. She grasped his hand and smiled her recognition. Without fawning, he shared his feeling of delight over her performance and strolled along with the crowd.

"Oh, let's go this way." she chortled happily and, skipping, led him into the garden. A gibbous moon had arisen and lit their way among the old English rose bushes that Skene had nurtured, trying to recreate what he loved most about the Motherland. In a grove of maples bordering the garden, Skene's gardener had cut some walking trails. Persons in the grove were concealed from the sight of those in the mansion. The odor of Phoebe in her crisp, starched dress mingled with those of nature as they walked these paths slowly. She hummed a bit of the aria and grasped his arm, leaning engagingly against him. He slipped an arm around her waist and drew her close, noting her trim form beneath the billow of clothing. She did not resist as he buried his face in her hair and drank in the mild scent of her cologne. Her lips found his as she clasped hands behind his neck and pressed him down. He had never been in such Elysian Fields before and was surprised by the gentle strength of her grasp. Those same hands, smooth and graceful, how could they express such urgency?

When their lips unlocked, they were both trembling, he drawing short breaths close to her ear. "Phoebe, my bonnie one." he blurted. She caressed his cheek, pushing him slightly away from her ear whose lobe was now moist and throbbing. "Such a prodigal lad you are and charming," she giggled lightly, but continued to hold him close.

The commotion back in the mansion and cries of "Phoebe, where are you?" by several breathless young women being pursued by a young officer running down the rose path broke into their rapture and they returned to the party.

*   *   *

"Tell me", Jenny inquired.

"It's the Colonel. He's been shot and captured somewhere in the wilderness down lake!" She moaned softly. "And I've been flirting here with Gentleman Johnny while Charles does his duty. Wretched woman I am! Must go to him at once. He will need care."

"But won't the soldiers find him and bring him back?"

"Not before morning and I fear for his wounds and what other punishments the rebels may inflict. No, I will go immediately."

Jenny thought for a moment. "But you can't go out into that dangerous forest alone. I will go with you. At least I know which tracks will keep you from being lost."

Lady Charlotte smiled wanly. "You are a true friend, Jenny. We will have several of Charles's trusted men with us."

After Lady Charlotte slipped into her bag the .50 caliber wheel lock pocket pistol that her husband had provided, the two stepped out a side door of the mansion and into the night.

22

British General St. Leger pressed his siege on Fort Stanwix. The rebels were proving most troublesome and stubborn to hold up his advance meant to harass the colonials south of the lakes, then join Burgoyne's larger army. Reports of a rebel force advancing up the Mohawk River to reinforce the fort defenders was unnerving and a dispatch from St. Leger for help now lay like a ticking time bomb on Burgoyne's battle map.

Caleb roused Rob early the day after the entertainment. "We've got work to do and miles to go. Get the horses ready. We leave as soon as possible." This was the last that Rob wanted to hear after his evening tryst with Phoebe in the garden.

Slinging bridles on the horses in the barn, Rob rubbed his eyes in disbelief when he heard redcoats assembling in the street being loudly commanded to move quickly north towards Fort Ti.

"Where are they going?" he asked a teamster.

"Some damn rebels hijacked Gentleman Johnny's wagons and he's mad as a hornet. When our boys find them they'll sure wish they'd stayed home."

Rob saddled the horses and led them to the Elkinton compound where a force of 100 Tories and Indians were preparing to move. Caleb exited the house and mounted, calling out to his Tory officers and Indian leaders to have their companies follow on. Rob grew more confused when Caleb led them south instead of joining the redcoats leaving in the other direction.

"Where are we going?" he demanded impatiently as he rode beside Caleb.

"West to the Mohawk River, then to Fort Stanwix". He would say nothing more until they reached the Indian towns along the river where he tried to enlist more mercenaries. A few natives agreed to sign on, but squabbles between the Mohawks and Abinakis soon made Caleb wish he had fewer of them and more Tories. Undaunted, he pushed on rapidly, hoping to bolster St. Leger's troops stalled at Fort Stanwix.

Rounding a bend in the river, Rob noted a faint smell of smoke. Sweet and pungent, it was unlike that of the Mohawk towns they had passed. He laid a hand on Caleb's arm to halt and be on guard, but could not clearly explain his caution.

Caleb shook him off. "We have no time to waste. We are many miles short of the fort."

As they pushed on, Caleb grew aware that his Mohawks were melting away from the river into the woods. A Tory subaltern rode up, eyes wild, with the news that the Mohawks were deserting quickly. "Fully a third of our force is now gone, sir, and those remaining say they will go no further."

"Damn savages!", Caleb cursed. He turned to Rob. "We'll stop here briefly while I go back to convince them. Come with me." They rode quickly to find the Mohawks mumbling in a group beside the river.

Before Caleb could address them, they grew silent, casting eyes here and there into the woods and down the river road they had just traveled. Rob read the signs of panic and asked the Mohawk leader what was the matter.

"There are other soldiers near who are hidden from us and we do not know their intent." The leader was clearly as spooked as his men.

Caleb scoffed at the news and asked why their scouts had not seen anything. The Mohawk's eyes rolled. "Scouts have not returned from the wood or ahead of us. They have gone to the wind and tell us nothing."

For the first time Caleb had the sense that something serious was wrong. He turned in his saddle to consult his Tory lieutenants when musket fire boomed from the woods to their rear. The Mohawk leader dropped, clawing at his breast where a crimson flower had suddenly bloomed. This single volley brought chaos and the redmen fled, splashing into the woods across the river, leaving the Tories unprotected. Hemmed in by the river and narrow road, Caleb immediately saw the folly in resisting. A rebel contingent led by a Green Mountain captain quickly captured the remaining Tories and escorted them to a farmhouse where a rebel force five times the size of Caleb's was resting, eating their dinner. The odor that had twitched Rob's nose was pork fat, now seen sizzling over open fires.

Caleb and Rob were marched to the farmhouse that the commander of the rebels used as his headquarters.

The swarthy colonial in blue uniform was bent over a map with several aides. As he moved around the table, he limped, but showed no symptom of pain. When Caleb and Rob were presented, he turned, his scowling facial expression turning to surprise. Rob was stunned and speechless as he looked into the eyes of General Benedict Arnold.

Arnold ignored Caleb and addressed Rob. "It seems, young man, that you prefer working both sides of the street. You must know how we deal with turncoats?"

"Sir", Caleb interrupted, "this man is a non-combatant who serves as my translator. In a sense he is my prisoner, having been captured on the battlefield at Hubbardton. Do what you will with me as your prisoner, but let this man go."

Arnold turned to Caleb for the first time. "Ah, my friend, you have an honorable streak, despite that green uniform you wear. Tell me, how did you expect to help your British friends with that handful of men at your command? We, too, are on our way to Stanwix just in time to drive your redcoats out of New York."

Caleb met the sarcastic implication with a steady eye. "That is your duty, sir, as mine was in reverse."

Arnold said no more and turned back to his maps. Over his shoulder, he remarked, "Major Elkinton, you will sign a statement that you and your men will not combat my colonial troops and will return on parole to your home. I am too busy to feed and care for Tory prisoners at this time. Perhaps in the future I will have the honor of meeting you again."

Caleb swallowed his pride and signed, knowing that to protest would endanger his men for no reason. As his now shrunken band turned back down the Mohawk River, it began to rain, soon drenching them. The storm continued to pelt them all the way back to Skenesboro.

*   *   *

Jenny and Lady Charlotte, accompanied by two menservants and a trusted Abenaki guide, rode north in darkness. They made good time in reaching the ambush site, despite gust-driven rain which soaked them through. Hopes of the servants for stopping and seeking some shelter were dashed by Lady Charlotte who instructed the guide to continue, following the ruts of the captured wagons which led off to the east, deeper into the forest. In short order, it was apparent that they were lost when the guide discovered that the wagon tracks had disappeared, the result of a wrong turn in the dark. Plunging ever deeper into thick forest whose lower branches felt like ominous wet claws slashing at their faces, Lady Charlotte finally called for a halt until sunrise and to look for whatever shelter they could best get in a copse of dense hemlock. Unsatisfied, the guide continued on only to return with the news that around the bend, just ahead was a military blockhouse where they could shelter. A crackling in the underbrush unnerved them momentarily, but dismounted, they squished behind him with torches and confronted a massive ghostly structure. Jenny wrinkled her nose, picking up the scent of wood smoke. The blockhouse had not been long abandoned as a brief investigation revealed warm embers inside on the main floor. As Jenny laid her wet cloak in a dark corner, she suddenly recoiled with a scream upon meeting a pair of staring, but unseeing eyes. A dead man was seated against the wall. He had suffered a massive chest wound from a musket ball and was still warm.

The guide confirmed that the man was a Mohawk and with the help of the servants, dragged the corpse outside and laid it in a ditch behind the blockhouse. It was clear that the Mohawks had just been here, perhaps retreating when they heard the approach of the search party. Was that crackling they heard the exit of the redmen? And would they be back? Lady Charlotte told them all that they would have to take their chances and find a dry spot on the second floor platform, but wisely posted a guard with a musket by the door. Sleep was difficult on the log floor in wet clothes among the old blankets left by passing troops and others, but slumber they did.

Morning broke, clear and cool. Their guide retraced his steps and found the ruts of the captured wagons. Jenny noted that they twisted south and from memory of Caleb's maps knew that the Castleton road could not be far off. As she predicted, in short order they broke through to a much-traveled thoroughfare. The wagon tracks were harder to follow now, but recent cuts on the grassy edges led them to believe that the captured were headed for Hubbardton.

*   *   *

Justice had convinced the rebel leader to stay on the Castleton road where they could make better time and avoid any bloody-back rescue party. "There be a Frenchie settlement off the way where we get some good food and medical help for the colonel." Penfield was now moaning with pain in the lead wagon. Justice had other reasons, too. That dark-eyed Canuck promised to be a tasty morsel once they got to the settlement.

23

Depressed, Caleb dragged his small band of Tories back into Skenesboro. He would have to report directly to Burgoyne what had happened and dreaded it. By now the stalemate at Fort Stanwix and the news that Arnold was on his way to blunt St. Leger would have reached the commander's ears. What he hated most was the certain derision that would come from the redcoated regulars. Their officers always looked down their noses at his Tory troops who had adapted to Indian warfare, abandoning the rigid English military tradition of masses of men choreographed in advancing shoulder-to-shoulder lines.

The commander was not in good humor. In fact, he was beside himself with anger and dread. The rescue party sent to retrieve the women had skirmished with renegade Mohawks and returned empty-handed. To say nothing about his missing Lady Charlotte, the Fort Stanwix standoff had further rattled his confidence. Fears of a rebel noose starting to tighten around his army were beginning to sink in.

Caleb ate crow. "My humblest apologies for failing in my mission, sir.", he uttered, head bowed. "I seek your leave to return to my home where the Blair family awaits me."

Burgoyne turned and stared out the window while his aides shifted uncomfortably. "Major, I have bad news for you. The elder Blair girl, Jenny, is with Lady Charlotte. They left here to seek her wounded husband late captured by the rebels. A rescue party sent north has found neither of them."

Stunned, Caleb looked at each of the aides who averted his eyes, nodding with what their general had just said. "What! Why was she permitted to go?"

"They did not seek permission, but left on their own accord." An aide stepped forward to reassure Caleb that they were still searching.

"No, you are delaying and have no real plan, do you?" Reading the blank stares told him the answer.

"My men shall immediately leave to find them. I will need with me the officer who has conducted the search thus far."

Burgoyne turned suddenly. "No, Major, you are needed here to prepare for our move southward to Albany. St. Leger's delay has made our position more vulnerable. We march tonight and hope soon to join General Clinton's forces moving upriver."

Caleb's eyes widened, but he had the presence to come to attention, salute and make for the door. No one stopped him. He brushed past Rob, grabbed the reins to his horse, mounted and galloped off to the Elkinton compound. Phoebe would surely know more about this than a roomful of regulars.

*　　*　　*

Tomsoc observed the rebel force long before it reached the Acadian settlement and had alerted Ian and Josh to their arrival. His lips curled as he told them that the scoundrel, Justice, was among them.

"What do you think they want?" Ian was disgusted by yet another incursion by armed troops.

"They appear to have a wounded man in one of the wagons."

"Then, we will make room. You say that they number less than 30 men and there are Mohawks among them?"

"No Mohawks, but they are militia, not continentals."

Ian grunted, not liking any of this. Josh knew that the presence of Justice among them spelled real trouble, recalling that the blackguard was playing both sides in this conflict to a fare thee well. With Ian's permission, he would stay out of sight until they had come and gone. Before long the rebel train lumbered into their compound and the rebel commander went to the inn and confronted Ian, saying that he intended to stay several days and needed medical help with his captive.

"And who is he?", Ian queried suspiciously.

"A redcoat officer for whom I intend to seek ransom. I've sent a man ahead under white flag to express terms at Fort Ti. He will join us here in two days."

"And bring the wrath of a lobsterback rescue party upon us." Ian exploded.

"That I cannot say, but in any event after the transaction we will be gone."

Ian rubbed his scar and growled. "Better we look at this wounded one right away. Have your men bring him in here. The women will tend to him as they do our hurt people."

The colonel, now running a fever, was laid in a back room where it was coolest and Amalie and No Hair tried to make him comfortable. After being washed and given water, he went into a coma. Amalie viewed the situation with alarm and charged past the resting militia towards the distant cowsheds where she knew Josh and Tomsoc were staying out of sight. They would know other remedies to help the wounded colonel. No Hair would know their proper administration.

Under their care, the colonel improved and, as the rebel leader hoped, negotiations with the British at Fort Ti looked promising. But the very next day, Lady Charlotte's entourage entered the Acadian settlement. They dismounted by the inn and asked a woman lugging water who lived here.

"Now what?", growled Ian as he limped out to meet the women.

"I am looking for my husband, Colonel Penfield, who may have passed here with serious wounds inflicted by his captors. I intend to find and care for him."

The rebel lieutenant gazing over Ian's shoulder smelled trouble and moved to neutralize this intrusion. "He is here in this inn and being cared for by these Acadian women. He will be released to the commander of Fort Ti this very week."

Lady Charlotte gave him a look of utter contempt, handed her reins to her servant and stormed past the man. When she found her Charles, she broke down whimpering and clasped his hand, giving his brow a gentle caress. Recovering quickly, she looked his caregivers up and down, asking what had been done to heal the wounds. Amalie and No Hair, in broken language, explained, giving hope that the worst was behind him and that he would be ready to move in a few days. Jenny had now joined her and after the two acknowledged that proper care was being given, marched back to the rebel officer.

"You will turn my husband over to me immediately and I will take him to Skenesboro for medical attention by British surgeons."

The rebel smiled slyly. "That would cost you more than you would care to know. He is to be ransomed by rules that our combating armies have established and will be escorted to the fort at my convenience."

Lady Charlotte was deeply troubled, but would not beg. "Then I will go with him to see that you keep your promise." Surprise and dread appeared alternatively on the young lieutenant's face as he angrily shook his head to this idea.

24

Amalie, whose task also was to assure cleanliness of the wounded, hoisted the chamber pot and made her way to the outhouse behind the cowshed. As she turned the corner and became out of sight of the inn, a stranger blocked her path, smiling triumphantly. "See what I got here, little lady." He held up a small purse, giving it a shake to indicate the contents. "They's hard gold and it be yours for the taking." Amalie bowed her head and kept walking. Justice jangled the coins, then produced an inscribed silver cross and laid a hand on her shoulder. Quick as a snake, she whirled and cast the entire contents of the pot over the grinning Lothario.

"No way to treat a man!" Justice howled in anger and groped Amalie roughly. She squirmed, but could not break his grasp. A commanding voice behind them boomed. "Unhand her, you charlatan, or you lose your guts!" Ian held an ugly looking officer's horse pistol, primed and ready to fire. Justice hissed, but backed away, letting Amalie scamper back to the inn. The lame man holding the pistol was much smaller than he, but knew there was no argument with that weapon.

"Thy stink insults the nose" Ian grimaced. "Get back to your teamsters and leave our women be. We have none who are light-o-loves that you seek." Justice eyed the pistol, then the fury in Ian's scarred face and thought better of not obeying. Turning, he made for his wagon, all the while covered by Ian's pistol. Stooping, Ian picked up the crucifix dropped by Justice in the confrontation.

Upon returning to the inn, Ian could not stifle a guffaw, as he faced Amalie. "Aye, Amalie, ye did the proper thing, lass. There was never a better use for your bucket!" Extending his hand, he urged Amalie to take the cross. "You must have this for your trouble."

No Hair, standing nearby, let out a mournful cry, snatched the icon from Ian and pressed it to her breast. Amid tears and mewing, she identified the inscriptions as those of Father Henri. Amalie put her arms around the Abenaki's shoulders to quiet her distress.

Ian was dumbfounded. "Are you sure of this, No Hair?" She nodded, eyes closed.

"Could this be the man who confronted Father Henri on the road?"

"No, no", she mewed and continued to finger the cross. Ian thought for a moment. The teamster must have obtained it in trade, but he now knew that murderous thieves still stalked about somewhere in this wilderness.

Neither threats nor pleading by the rebel commander would have any effect on Lady Charlotte and in the end he agreed to take her, but not her entourage. Jenny and the servants would stay until the rebels left after which Tomsoc would accompany her back to Skenesboro. Before departing for Fort Ti, Lady Charlotte drew Jenny aside and, with no one aware, cleverly passed the wheel-lock pistol into her friend's travelling bag, saying "You may have need of this. Can you fire a pistol? Jenny's eyes widened, but nodded her head affirmatively. "Be most careful, Jenny and Godspeed home to Skenesboro"

Justice knew that his stay in the settlement was nearly over. While lounging under a maple, he caught sight of Amalie out of the corner of his eye. She was bound for the cowshed with a milk pail in hand. He smirked and took off at an angle to cut her off. She had nearly reached her goal when two burley arms emerged from the brush, embraced her and pushed her into the undergrowth. Stunned and frightened, she grasped a stout branch and beat at her attacker who easily fended off the blows, grinning malevolently. Out of nowhere, Tomsoc suddenly appeared, a pitchfork in hand which he drove deeply into Justice's buttocks and leg. The giant howled, clutched his wound and forgot about Amalie. Tomsoc prepared to skewer again a more vulnerable spot as Justice begged for mercy.

"No, no!" Amalie screamed, coming between the two.

Tomsoc, eyes blazing, held back, but pinned his quarry against a tree trunk. As Tomsoc turned to look at Amalie, Justice came to his senses and dashed nimbly away, making for the militia band, blood oozing down his trouser leg. Tomsoc led Amalie by a circuitous route back to the inn, then, pail in hand, returned to the cowshed for milking. This did not escape Justice's notice. Eyes smoldering eyes with hate, he determined to get revenge if it was the last thing he did.

Having seen quite enough of Justice, the lieutenant released him and his teamsters on the pretense that his services had helped the new republic. Ian limped out in search of him and his band to ensure that the troublemaker was sent packing immediately, but found no one. They had already slipped away on horseback, leaving their wagons and baggage behind. "Good riddance!" he spat out to no one.

With Justice gone, Josh emerged from hiding and was surprised to find Jenny still at the inn. After hearing what had been decided, he was skeptical of anyone moving down the Castleton Road in these troubled times. A beautiful young woman like Jenny, travelling alone with little protection, would be extremely vulnerable to capture and harm. He included the name of Justice to this danger, but the others were sure that by now he was riding hard for the protection of Skenesboro. The extra security Tomsoc offered might not be enough.

Over the next day, Amalie and Jenny became close as they assisted Josh and Lady Charlotte preparing the colonel for his journey. In casual conversation, Jenny dropped Rob's name and his ties with the Tories, Amalie and Josh could scarcely believe their ears, but were cheered at the good news of his safety.

"Oh, he is with Major Elkinton and in no danger." Jenny explained. "Further, he has reasons for staying in Skenesboro, one them being my sister, Phoebe." She smiled knowingly at Lady Charlotte. Amalie grew increasingly uncomfortable at this news and wished to hear no more of the conversation. Lady Charlotte, always astute, noticed and drew her out. Hoping to ease her concern for Rob, Jenny continued. "He isn't a Tory recruit, you know. Simply translates for my fiancé, Major Caleb Elkinton. He'll return here just as soon as the rebels leave the Hudson Valley."

Amalie wasn't so sure of anyone's safety anymore. Moreover, she now began to realize that the rough Acadian culture might be a disappointment for Rob after he had seen the rich and pampered lives of the Tories. This beautiful woman and most likely her sister Phoebe would turn any young man's head.

Seeing the dark conflict in Amalie's eyes, Lady Charlotte added gently, "I mean no offense, but those of us who are differently raised and privileged think different thoughts, not all of which are understood by others. I confess that I had never thought of the strength and mercy you have shown to us, your enemies, until now. But for me to become one of your family here in the wilderness would be impossible. Jenny, her sister Phoebe and I are sailing in a different sea than you and the waters will never meet. Rob will see this eventually and come to you, please believe me."

At this, Amalie bit her lip, but could not prevent the tears welling in her eyes. She wiped them on her sleeve as she turned to finish preparations for the wounded colonel's departure. Josh, quietly making the Colonel comfortable, overheard all the conversation and felt Amalie's pain. He had seen the strict class lines of the privileged and non-privileged at play in Cornwall and Boston. There was no reason to think that things were different out here on the edge of civilization despite all the rebel talk of freedom and equality. If Rob couldn't figure this out, he was determined to fill him in.

25

The colonial militia and the Penfields departed north the next day. Josh's concerns did not delay Jenny and her small entourage. The day was hot and humid as they rode south on the Castleton Road. But they made good time without the wagons and stopped only when their Abenaki guide urged them to take the shorter route through the forest where he knew of a spring for refreshing themselves and the horses. Jenny soon realized that it was the same track they had been on during the search and blanched at the thought of nearing the blockhouse again. She still had the horrid vision of those dead eyes of the savage staring back at her. Toward noon they neared the structure and dismounted, glad to be out of the saddle for a time.

The guide led the horses uphill some 100 yards to the spring which was gurgling out of moss-covered rocks. Tomsoc and the others sought the cool relief of the blockhouse interior, but Jenny refused to enter and followed the guide and horses. After slaking her thirst, she picked her way carefully down the slope. Before she reached the blockhouse, a grinning hulk with yellowed front teeth barred her way. Justice had prepared a neat trap. With the blockhouse entrance covered by teamster muskets and some renegade Mohawks surrounding the horses and guide, he could easily harvest this low-hanging fruit. After he was done with her, she would make him a fortune as part of his mobile brothel.

Jenny gasped in fear, but slid the wheel lock pistol from her garments and aimed it at Justice's chest. At a distance of five feet she would never miss. Surprised, Justice suddenly lost his confident look and licked his lips.

"Get out of my way." Jenny hissed and sprinted past him towards the fortress. But before she went 20 steps, a Brown Bess musket thundered from the underbrush and Jenny collapsed, the ounce weight ball tearing her insides.

"Who the hell fired?" screamed Justice as he swooped down at her side and pried the wheel lock out of her hand. But Justice was thwarted yet again. The beautiful body lay still. Arias would never more pass those gentle lips. Jenny was already dead.

Inside the blockhouse, the servants cringed with fear and confusion. Tomsoc ordered them to stay put while he left to investigate. Slipping out the entrance like a cougar, he rounded the corner, musket in hand, and confronted the sorry scene. Still bent over Jenny, Justice raised his head and yelled, "I didn't do it, I swear!" Tomsoc, in a fury, aimed his weapon, but was caught by two rounds from the teamsters before he could fire and dropped where he stood. Quick as a fox, Justice rolled aside and into the underbrush just as the Mohawks guarding the spring came crashing down the incline. For a time all seemed frozen in place, trying to understand what had happened. Justice came to first and emerged from the brush, stood over Tomsoc and nudged him with a toe of his boot. Tomsoc groaned and turned over to reveal a flesh wound on his neck and more serious bleeding from the hip. Justice thought for a time, then grinned. "Let's take those still shitting their pants in the blockhouse."

While he and the teamsters rounded up the servants, the Mohawks stood near Jenny's corpse, fingering their knives. Finally the leader held up his hand to the others, stooped swiftly and slit her scalp, front and rear. Putting his foot on her back, he tore savagely, removing her long, luxurious hair intact and, holding it for the others to see, proclaimed that it would bring a fine bounty.

Even Justice wasn't prepared for this and grimaced when the Mohawk leader thrust the scalp in his face. But always fast on his feet, Justice managed a nod of approval and, after checking Tomsoc's wounds, told the Mohawks to tie the wounded Abenaki on a horse for transport to the British camp. Beginning to smirk, Justice now had his alibi. Tomsoc would be his bargaining chip with the redcoats. The servants whimpered tearfully as they wrapped Jenny's body in the dirty cast-off blankets from the blockhouse and packed her onto a horse for return to Skenesboro.

"Where's your kinsman?" he yelled to the Mohawks. In the melee, the renegade Mohawks had forgotten about Lady Charlotte's guide. When the shooting began, they left him alone and piled down the slope to the fighting. Lingering only long enough to size up the scene, the guide had melted into the forest, making for Hubbardton in great haste. Justice got no answer, but gave the disappearance little thought. The guide must have been scared like the servants and even if he did surface later, who would believe anything he might say?

By the time they reached Skenesboro, Justice had a carefully concocted tale. He led the group by a side path to the farmhouse used by the British surgeons and requested they treat Tomsoc at once. Jenny's corpse was dumped on a litter to be fitted for observation by family and those who knew her. As an orderly unwrapped her body, a half dozen well-fed bedbugs fell to the floor and attempted to crawl out of the light. Each was then promptly stomped by the orderly with a sickening, bloody pop.

One of the British surgeons sent word to the Blairs at Elkinton's house with the tragic news. The Blairs were stunned by the report and refused to believe it. Caleb reacted as if struck by a club and, for the moment, could only stand mute, head on his chest. But after assuring the family that it may be only a rumor, he tore out the door looking for his horse. Rob was grooming the mare and didn't like the fire he saw in Caleb's eyes. "Come with me." he muttered. When Rob was slow to move, Caleb moaned, "Please!" They rode recklessly to the makeshift hospital where, upon seeing his mutilated love, Caleb collapsed and cried out in anguish, "Great God, Why?"

Rob was too muddled to think straight and dreaded the effect the tragedy would have on Phoebe and her parents. Then his eye caught the prostrate form in a corner and realized at once that it was Tomsoc. Rushing to the litter, he found the Abenaki alive although savagely wounded and in a coma. A surgeon who was trying to calm Caleb stepped near and related that Tomsoc would live, but recovery might be long and painful. Thinking fast now, Rob asked the surgeon how the two had gotten here. "One of the teamsters brought them in with the two menservants, saying they had been attacked by renegade Mohawks, one of them the wounded savage you see there." Then his lip curled. "He's the bastard responsible for the awful killing of the lass over there. We'll fix him up enough for the hanging."

Rob seethed at this conflicting tale, knowing that Tomsoc would never hurt anyone without cause. Struggling to stay calm, he asked, "This teamster, do you have a name?"

"A big man, rather disheveled, he left with two servants who called him Justice."

Rob's innards contracted. "Which direction did he take from here?

"Said he would dismiss the servants, then report to General Burgoyne's headquarters."

Rob glanced at Caleb who was still standing next to Jenny, his face pained beyond belief. He had not heard the surgeon's remarks, but Rob knew if he did not get Caleb away immediately, Tomsoc was likely a dead man. Unhurriedly, he eased the distraught Caleb out of the hospital, onto his horse and returned to the Elkinton home. Caleb's confirmation of Jenny's death served to increase the chaos and wailing of the family. The Reverend Blair immediately gathered his family in prayer attempting to console and to seek Almighty guidance.

Rob glanced at Phoebe's tearful face and wanted to take her away to a happier place, but quickly saw that she needed to remain, sharing her grieving with family and giving support to her mother. He, too, shared their misery, but clearly saw that he was an outsider. He nodded briefly and retired to the Elkinton garden, much troubled by what had happened. Still, he found it all too strange. "The servants," he suddenly remembered, "must find the servants."

He entered the Skene mansion by the back door. The serving folk were babbling in the kitchen. In shock, the two servants had difficulty telling of their ordeal, yet were grateful for having kept their hair. Rob listened carefully, before joining in with questions.

"You say that Jenny refused to go into the blockhouse where she might have had protection?"

"She was hot and thirsty and needed some of the springwater. She and our guide were the only ones who stayed outside. It was fearsome dark but cooler in the blockhouse and we thought they would join us after their water." Then there was a single shot and Tomsoc left to investigate. We heard more shots. Soon the big teamster barged in and told us we were lucky. He had the culprit who caused the trouble and he would make sure of safe passage back to Skene's mansion. He saved our lives."

Rob thought about this for a time. "But the first shot you heard couldn't have been Tomsoc's. He was with you in the blockhouse."

The servants hung their heads and looked at each other for support, but then agreed that Rob was right.

"And what happened to the guide?"

The shrugging shoulders told Rob what he wanted to know. Either the guide was dead or trying to get lost somewhere in the Green Mountains. And unless he were found to give account, Tomsoc would surely face the gallows.

A commotion in front of the mansion caused them all to rush through the garden to see a drunken Mohawk proudly brandishing Jenny's scalp. Word soon spread like wildfire throughout the troops and the drunk was hauled up to Burgoyne's headquarters for orders to hang the culprit immediately. Burgoyne hesitated and, ever cautious, told his officers to confine the Mohawk. Before he could be led away, Phoebe came running up to Rob, having heard the awful news. Spotting the scalp, she let out a wail and needed his arm for support. He embraced her and turned her away, then led her to the garden and a bench where she continued sobbing. Shuddering in his arms, Phoebe told him that the news had pushed her mother over the edge. She had moaned incessantly since learning of her daughter's fate and Burgoyne's physician could do nothing for her. Only Phoebe, with arms around her mother's shoulders could staunch the weeping. Recovering her composure, Phoebe said she must get back to the family. Rob understood and walked her back to the Elkinton home. But before leaving the Skene mansion, he spotted Justice emerging from

Burgoyne's quarters among a group of officers. "That's a bit odd," he thought, "a mere teamster reporting to some pretty high up people." What he didn't know was that Burgoyne's staff had just been informed of rich caches of food and fodder in Bennington, a town on the edge of the Green Mountains.

26

Amalie's hands ached after filling a second milk pail from the settlement's few lactating cows. She put one aside for family consumption, reserving the other for nourishment of the newborn calves. Weaning the newborn from the mother's teat was not always easy as the maternal bond was powerful. But much milk was lost by having suckling calves over-engorging or roughing up the mother. This resulted in much milk loss and the possibility of infection. The tried and true technique was to let the newborn get the smell of the warm milk in a pail, then immerse a human hand in the vital nourishment. With the other hand the calf's nose could be dunked in, all the while providing one of the submerged fingers as a bogus teat that the hungry calf would eagerly accept. After initiating the sucking reflex on the finger, milk would be drawn in and, with luck, the newborn would learn to start regular drinking. The finger could be slowly withdrawn, effectively breaking the young's reflex pattern. But it was not always successful and often required several attempts, especially after a day's hiatus. Despite an often-ravaged finger from the calf's eager sucking and emerging teeth, Amalie was both patient and very good with this weaning process. Further, she loved the close contact with her charges and was amused by their unfettered energy and antics.

This morning was no different and her young pupils had done well. The pail she held between her knees was nearly gone and she rose from the kneeling position, putting out her hand on the bedding for balance. From the corner of her eye she detected movement in the straw not a foot away. A blotched pattern of smooth scales slid easily past the pail, nearly touching her hand. Recoiling in horror, she sent the pail flying and let out a scream.

Josh rushed into the shed to investigate and found Amalie wide-eyed and trembling by the door. "What happened? Are you hurt?"

"It was one of those snakes that steals milk from our cows. And a big one!" Her voice was high and lips were aquiver.

Josh went to the calf pen and retrieved the empty pail, spotting the tail end of the snake slithering out the back. Amalie was suddenly beside him grasping his arm. "There it goes." she gasped.

"You silly girl, Amalie." he said, good-naturedly. He handed her the pail and told her not to worry. "That snake is neither a viper nor a milk thief. That milk tale is nonsense. No way can it suckle a cow! And can you imagine any of our cattle allowing it?" He embraced Amalie until she stopped trembling and felt less distracted.

"How can you be sure, Josh?"

He suddenly realized that a warm flush was enveloping him, urging that the embrace continue with more vigor. With considerable effort, he checked himself, his mind stumbling, trying to concentrate on her question. Finally, he cleared his throat.

"Oh, its best not to mess with anything that size 'cause it may turn on you." He struggled to catch his breath. "The serpent has no venom. Feeds on those mice that run through our straw."

She slowly left his embrace a bit embarrassed, but flashed him a bright smile which seemed to say something more than "Thank you."

*   *   *

Despite the interruptions of war, the Acadians continued to work their lands, knowing full well that neither redcoats nor rebels would ease the oncoming challenges of a Vermont winter. Sweating profusely and glad for the temporary lull in fieldwork, Amalie watched the wagon loaded with hay rumble off to the barns. Seeking relief from the sun beside a nearby hay cock, she savored the slight breeze wafting up off the lake. Josh, drenched in sweat, plunked the gourd dipper deep into the pail of spring water, lifted it and drank heavily, returning twice more to slake his thirst. Satisfied, he scooped up yet another round and handed it to Amalie who eagerly gulped it down. As they both settled back comfortably on the hay, she murmured "Merci" and closed her eyes. Josh couldn't help but notice the soiled and wet cheeks that were streaked with more than sweat.

"Tell me, Amalie. It's about Rob, isn't it?" She sniffed a little and turned her head away, nodding to the question.

"Ah, he'll be back, you'll see." She turned suddenly and held him close. The pressure of her body made him feel good all over and he wrapped his arms around her and clung for a long time, his lips in her hair.

"Josh, you won't ever leave us, will you?" she whispered into his neck. Josh relaxed his arms and lifting her head, kissed the soiled brow.

"Don't know." he muttered, taking her hands in his. "Sort of depends on who the victors are, Tories or rebels."

"Feel my hands, Josh. They're rough and callused. Rather like some farm animal that just works every day through its life. What man would prefer to hold them when delicate, unspoiled hands might stroke his cheek?" Josh remained silent, but continued to clasp her hands, gently rubbing the palms.

"We aren't any of us perfect, Amalie. Look at the ugly burns on my neck. They're enough to scare off a witch, but I can't erase them. You and your people have shown me that it doesn't matter what I look like."

Amalie leaned and caressed his neck scars, smiling, then kissed both his cheeks, lingering long until Josh gently disengaged, heart racing at her physical closeness. Both silently acknowledged their special love for each other as brother/ sister soul mates. But Josh could not help noticing a twist of agitation in his gut as to what might happen if he stayed much longer at the settlement. Filled with regret, he suddenly knew that his time with the Acadians would soon over. Looking up, he saw with some relief the empty hay wagon returning for the next load.

27

The Abenaki guide knew his territory well and moved swiftly and silently through the forest. Only once had he stopped and, climbing a large white pine had stayed hidden, listening for human pursuers. Male cicadas droned their mating buzz, making other sounds hard to discern for even the guide's experienced ears. Finally, deciding he heard only forest sounds, he quickly shimmied down and continued his pace. Four hours later he broke out of the trees onto the military highway and soon was at the Acadian settlement. No Hair's eyes became dark with recalled terror at the news and she moaned most awfully for the beautiful lady now dead. Josh and Amalie also recoiled in horror, but knew at once that Tomsoc, if alive, had to be rescued. If only Lady Charlotte could hear the Abenaki guide's account, she would be their best advocate. Recovering, it was No Hair who knew that Rob, who might still be in Skenesboro, would be the key to Tomsoc's survival. Against Ian's wishes, she left at once to find Rob, inform him of the guide's tale and the impending intervention of Lady Charlotte. Josh and the Abenaki guide departed for Fort Ti to find Lady Charlotte.

Meanwhile, at the British camp, pressure was building to hang both Tomsoc and the renegade Mohawk. But much to Justice's chagrin, officers were advising Burgoyne to spare the lives of the native Americans as these valuable mercenaries might mutiny and melt away in anger. The British needed all their support if the rumors of growing rebel strength were accurate. This threat now weighed heavily in his decisions. Despite his revulsion and sorrow about the scalping, the commander ordered that no Indians would hang until he had taken Albany after which he would turn the accused over to Tory authorities for prosecution. The renegade Mohawk was to be imprisoned and Tomsoc soon to join him after recovery from wounds. Rob's dilemma now was to keep Tomsoc away from the wrath of Caleb who, though drowned in sorrow, would soon be looking to exact revenge. For now, Caleb kept to himself and would see no one.

Josh and the guide waited nervously on the Champlain shore for the redcoat escort to take them into Ft. Ti. Recalling his last encounters at the fort, Josh was full of apprehension. The huge black in British garb striding towards them did nothing to alleviate his fears, but closer scrutiny revealed that he was, the same soldier who had sprung him from the prison. The fort commander eyed them both suspiciously until Lady Charlotte arrived and Colonel Penfield verified their status. Lady Charlotte groaned at the shocking news, lamenting that she should never have separated from Jenney. She and the Colonel begged the commander to send Josh and the guide to Skenesboro at once. He immediately ordered that the two and veteran paddlers depart with a courier bearing Penfield's request to release Tomsoc. To escape detection from General Lincoln's rag-tag but strengthening rebel militia, they were escorted by a squad of soldiers dressed as natives. One of them was the giant black by the name of name Atticus. As they pushed off, Atticus shared with Josh that his friend, Jeremy, was improved, but remaining in hospital.

*   *   *

No Hair moved easily into the Royal Army camp, shunned or ignored by both redcoats and Mohawks. When Rob returned to the hospital, he was astonished to find her sitting next to Tomsoc. Upon hearing her report, he now knew that Justice's tale was a total fabrication, but that no one in the Burgoyne camp would believe otherwise. He had to confide in someone. Perhaps Phoebe could calm Caleb and open him to some reason. She listened to Rob's defense of Tomsoc, not wanting any further discussion, but finally agreed to tell Caleb of Rob's concerns.

Caleb had secreted himself in his study in the Elkinton mansion. The Tory looked wretched as Rob was ushered in for the private conference. "You want to tell me something?" he mumbled, never rising or diverting his gaze from the window. Rob hesitated, but then poured out his plea to save his friend's life. Caleb said nothing for a time, then rose and confronted him. "I thought you had a stronger spine, lad. Even began to consider you as my friend, but I now see that your loyalties are elsewhere with the natives and the metis from which you came. You'll always be a grubber of soil, happy with that hardscrabble life that you left. I should have known better. Blood is always the ultimate glue." He returned to his chair and put his head in his hands.

"You may go or stay in our camp. You are no longer my captive, but if you leave, you go alone. Before this war is done, I'll see that savage friend of yours dangle from a rope. Now please leave me be."

Rob turned to exit and nearly collided with Phoebe coming through the door. She saw the look on his face and touched his arm as they passed. He kept going as the door closed behind her. Returning to the hospital, he confided to his friends that the British would not hang Tomsoc, but as long as he remained in the British camp he was still in danger. Rob promised to stay by him until he was well and plan an escape. But his mind and heart raged in conflict. He must free Tomsoc, but with Phoebe still in Skenesboro he knew he could not leave.

Tension in the British ranks increased daily. Rob stayed out of the way, but noted that Justice was a regular visitor to Burgoyne's headquarters. He learned from the ensign who had reported Colonel Penfield's mishap that Justice was warning the commander and his staff that unless they advanced on Albany soon, his army would be outnumbered by rebel forces. In short order, on the advice of his war council, Burgoyne finally dispatched troops south, first to Fort Edward, then into a devilish thicket of obstacles left by General Schuyler's retreating rebels. These delaying tactics proved to be the redcoat's worst nightmare, causing them to creep rather than march the few miles to Albany.

Just as the Royal Army commander prepared to join his vanguard and vacate Skenesboro, Josh and his undercover guard arrived from Fort Ti. He wasted no time finding Rob at the hospital and was relieved to learn that Tomsoc was cared for and healing. Leaving Atticus and his bogus Mohawks at the hospital, the two friends sought Burgoyne's chief aide to request a meeting with the commander. After reading Lady Charlotte's letter describing Tomsoc's innocence and Colonel Penfield's endorsement of clemency, Gentleman Johnny heard them out and ordered that Tomsoc remain in hospital until he could travel, then be placed in the custody of Josh who would return him to the Acadians.

"You", he looked directly at Rob, "will report to Major Elkinton and prepare to join the army now marching on the Hudson." For the first time both Josh and Rob noticed that Caleb had silently entered the room and stood at attention by the door. Rob's mouth opened, then quickly closed. Burgoyne immediately arose signaling the end of the discussion and joined a knot of officers at a map near the window through which poured a languishing August afternoon sun.

Returning to the hospital, they shared their information with Tomsoc who accepted his good fortune in the usual stoic manner. Atticus and his fellow soldiers were gone, having already been ordered to move south with the army. Burgoyne, for once, was moving with alacrity.

As the three friends made preparation to return to Hubbardton, Rob grew silent. That Rob was conflicted was most evident to Josh who drew his friend aside. "What's wrong? Are you not coming back to the settlement with us?"

"No. I've decided to stay with the army."

Josh was flabbergasted. "Why . . . why would you do that?" Rob shrugged and turned away.

Josh continued. "You never were any part of this army. All you have to do is disappear into the woods and return to your father. It's easy. I know because that's what I did to get away from the Bartons. It's clear that the Tory officer who took you has washed his hands of you. What else is holding you, the Tory lass?"

Rob nodded. All the images of his new life in Skenesboro suddenly sped through his brain. The clothes, the music and dancing, the genteel culture. His now ragged and unkempt friendship with Caleb and especially Phoebe. "No, I don't want to go back", he mumbled.

Josh eyed him severely. "You're a fool, Rob. Precious as she may be, that young woman and a life of idle comfort is not what you were made for. Your father needs you to run the inn and Amalie who loves you waits patiently for your return."

Rob whirled in a fury. "If you think all that is so good, why don't you just take my place? Amalie has always had eyes for you and all my relatives think you are essential to our settlement." With that, he turned to leave, but Josh caught his arm.

"Rob, my friend, you are as trapped here as I was in Boston. The worst of it is you don't realize what you've got. Denying your upbringing and what it has done for you will haunt for the rest of your life."

Rob turned to No Hair, seeking support, but met only a cold stare of disapproval and a garbled French and Abenaki incantation of dire things to come followed by sorrowful mewing. Tomsoc, in the corner, was holding his bowed head in his hands. Rob left without another word and made his way to the Elkinton mansion.

He walked slowly to let his anger subside and paused before entering, hearing only the servants' rising voices lamenting about how the army's departure was affecting their lives. Not wanting to get into the discussion, he went round back to the garden. Off to the side seated in a shady bower were Caleb and Phoebe, she leaning very close and holding his hand. For the first time, sharp pangs of jealousy struck him dumb. But they had not seen him and he withdrew in turmoil and doubt about what he chose to leave and what might come next.

28

Several days later, Josh, Tomsoc and No Hair returned to the settlement. Finding Ian alone in his chamber, Josh told him of his plans to leave the settlement. Ian groaned at the news and begged Josh to remain. "No", Josh was firm." I have been well treated here and will miss you as my family, but other life beckons. No longer do I fear my masters in Boston. They have not found me, nor will they, even if that villain, Justice, tries to pursue me or returns to the Bartons with news of finding me here."

Ian sighed again. "Josh, I may have lost my only son to this war and I don't wish to lose you. You are as close to another son as I will ever have."

"I know, my friend, but Rob will return soon, I'm sure." Josh rose to leave, then turned and embraced the older man for a last time. "Please tell everyone that I wish them well, but do not let them search for me. I leave tonight by way of the military road." He went to his room where he was packed and provisioned with sufficient food to carry him for several days, then stepped off on the road going south.

*   *   *

Caleb and his diminished force of Tories moved south at a snail's pace. Albany was some 45 miles from Fort Edward, now in British hands, but a single day's travel on horseback over nearly level ground. Schuyler was effectively constipating their movement, both men and supplies, with his clever delaying tactics. Felled trees blocked the single road and bridges over creeks and marshes had to be rebuilt. Burgoyne, making only one mile a day, cursed his lack of horse for the Hessians who might have been able to outflank the rebels. Caleb and Rob labored mightily with the remaining

Tory band to help clear the way, cursing the hordes of deer flies and mosquitos hovering to take blood meals from man and beast.

Dire news reached Burgoyne that General St. Leger was now rapidly retreating towards Canada after having been mauled and frightened at Fort Stanwix and Oriskany by General Herkimer and Benedict Arnold, who had just arrived from Philadelphia. Burgoyne pondered, "Where was Clinton? Not a word on his progress up the Hudson from New York as the plan had anticipated. Couriers sent south were not returning. Food and fodder were already running out despite the stores at the end of Lake George. If only Penfield were here. Perhaps his lines were getting too stretched? And what of this brigand called Justice, who was telling the staff that huge stores of guns and supplies were available in Bennington just for the taking?"

"Yes," he thought out loud, "the Hessians need something to do and so do these damned unreliable savages" He called Riedesel in and asked him to march a force of his men 20 miles southeast. Colonel Baum's Hessian regiment and a contingent of Tories and Mohawks left immediately.

*   *   *

Despite his brilliant retreat and the recent flood of enlistments by colonial farmers, General Philip Schuyler, rebel commander of the Northern Frontier, was in difficulty. Many of the politicians in Philadelphia held him responsible for the loss of Fort Ti and the flight from the Burgoyne's Royal army. General Horatio Gates, a schemer and self-promoter par excellence, wangled appointment as new commander to replace Schuyler. No matter that Gates himself, as a previous commander, had left the Champlain area forts with minimal support and defense plans. More problematic, he and Arnold, Schuyler's friend, had no liking for each other. Literally brushing aside both Schuyler and Arnold, he now took over command of the Continentals. Ironically, without much planning or consultation with the generals, his policy of hesitation appeared sound, letting Burgoyne, who continued to weaken, edge his way down the headwaters of the Hudson. When Arnold requested permission to attack, he and Gates had words that resulted in Arnold storming out of headquarters. Effectively sidelined, Arnold became ancillary to the rebel force, a brooding loose cannon, nursing yet another wound after having been passed over once again for a promotion by the politicians.

*   *   *

Caleb didn't like the sound of it. A courier had arrived with disturbing news from Baum that reinforcements were required. His force of Hessians had been stopped at a little river short of his objective, Bennington. There he had divided his force into small defensive units, but the rebels had infiltrated between them and were slowly overcoming their resistance. Burgoyne was again surprised. "Where could these rebels have come from?" he asked his adjutant. The blank stare was of no help. "That blackguard Justice never told us of any force that Baum could not handle." He looked at Riedesel. "Can you provide another regiment to help them?"

"Breymann is available, commander."

"Good. He shall start at once and make haste. You, Major Elkinton, will be Breymann's eyes and ears."

Caleb cobbled together a small contingent of Tories and reported with Rob in tow to Colonel Breymann.

The Hessian didn't seem all that eager to plunge into the wilderness, but was soon ready with several cannon to rescue Baum. They made slow progress given the continued rain and poor road east. The first indication of real trouble was the appearance of mercenary Mohawks splashing toward them, in a hurry to return to the main army. Caleb soon learned that Baum was completely surrounded in the redoubt he had hastily constructed on a little hill overlooking the waters of Waloomsoc Creek. Much to Caleb's chagrin, Breymann hesitated upon hearing this news and consulted his map. "But we must attack at once, sir," cried Caleb. "The rebels can be taken by surprise if we move rapidly." More Mohawks streamed past, followed by a few Tories who corroborated the bad news.

Breymann sent a probing force forward only to learn that surprise was now gone and a significant rebel group was bearing down on him. From a retreating Tory, Caleb and Rob found that Baum had been killed and most of his force captured by Warner's Green Mountain Boys. The Bennington excursion was over and Breymann wisely retreated after some initial exchange with the rebels. The rebels broke off, content with having won the day and several Hessian cannon.

*   *   *

Riedesal burst into Burgoyne's headquarters, lamenting his recent news from Breymann. "We are in retreat having failed to reach the supplies." The commander had never seen the stoic German general in such disarray. "And", Riedesal gasped, catching his breath, "my troops are now rebel prisoners. Baum is dead! My poor, good friend Baum!" He raised a hand to his forehead in despair.

Burgoyne clapped a hand on the German's shoulder. "I am most sorry. We shall see that his widow and children are well cared for. And what of Breymann and the cannon?"

"They will join us in hours, but they, too, have been hurt. The rebel force waiting vastly outnumbered us and fought with unusual vigor. This is not a good sign, Commander."

As they spoke, a horseman riding hard entered the British camp. He dismounted at Burgoyne's tent and presented himself to the adjutant. Dressed as a local farmer, he was delayed until his purpose and message was known. The adjutant immediately afforded him entry to Burgoyne who took the courier's written communication and read. He slowly sat down and continued to read. Finishing, he bowed his head and told the adjutant to assemble his war council. When gathered, he told them simply, "Howe is not coming." He hesitated, then continued. "He is on his way to Philadelphia to further harry that fox, Washington." The council was stunned and speechless, so Burgoyne continued. "We are now alone and have but two options. Either we cease advancing and remove to Ticonderoga or continue to Albany. Before sunset I want your assessments. Meet with me here first thing in the morning for the decision."

He retired to his tent, trying to understand what went wrong. He knew that he still had the best army in the British Empire and that in open combat under classical European warfare there was no equal. But these rebel farmers were crafty and, though inexperienced, could bleed his troops by a thousand razor cuts. And the debacle at Bennington was a deep saber wound. He looked at his map. Only 30 miles to Albany. A two-day march if it weren't for those damned rebel woodcutters. He would have to cross the Hudson soon at this place called Saratoga and when he did cross his communication with Fort Edward and Skenesboro would dwindle. The small food supplies available at Fort George would be inaccessible and the army would have to forage for everything. "Damn!" he grumbled then pounded the map. "Get me that whore monger, Justice", he shouted to his adjutant.

Justice appeared at once and stood disheveled before the commander. Burgoyne winced at his appearance, but bade him sit down. "What more can you tell me of the enemy's strength?" he asked sarcastically. Justice fidgeted for a moment, eyes darting about to the Adjutant.

"It don't look good, sir. That brigand Stark is fixin' to join Schuyler, fresh from the trouble at Bennington and they's building fortifications down the road to Albany."

"How many men does Schuyler have?" Burgoyne was impatient with this rouge.

"My people say about 6,000 when Stark gets to him."

Burgoyne eyed him sharply, then relaxed. "If your tale is correct, we'll need every soldier, but rebel militia of that size will hardly be a problem once we face them in open battle."

T' other thing is the rebel commander has been replaced with a new general called Gates," Justice continued. "Seems the politicians are sick of old Schuyler."

Burgoyne's eyebrows went up and he smiled smugly to his adjutant. "Oh, the former redcoat? That is good news indeed. We've seen the likes of him before."

Next morning the war council gathered. Many of the staff were uncomfortable about cutting their lifeline as most local farmers had scorched their farms and British raiding parties seeking provisions were constantly harried by continental sharpshooters. And rumors of rebels moving behind the army were discouraging to say the least. Burgoyne heard them out, but had already made up his mind. Turning to General Fraser, he said, "Select our best engineers to put a bridge of boats across the Hudson at Saratoga. Be sure that those cursed sharpshooters are kept at bay and we shall be chasing Gates no later than tomorrow."

Caleb was stunned yet again. At risk of questioning this order, he raised his voice. "What of the defenders at Fort Miller and Skenesboro, sir?" Burgoyne acted as if he had not heard and dismissed the council except for Fraser and the adjutant. Caleb remained, set on getting an answer. Burgoyne bade him come to the map table and laid a hand on his shoulder. "Major, I know you have lost your intended and fear for the lands you hold next to Skene's. You have my promise that when we drive Gates out of Albany and have broken the colonials, you and your Tories may return home and keep the rabble under foot. Right now I need you to double your efforts at rallying loyal families to support us with food and fodder. Our success will depend as much on you as on General Fraser here."

Caleb feared the worst for those few redcoats left in Skenesboro to protect the Blairs and the remaining Tory families, but nodded, knowing now that only a quick British victory would save the Loyalist cause. He would do his best for the fortunes of the army. Gathering Rob and his band of Tories, he told them to seek what mounts were available and prepare to scavenge neighboring farms, preferably with diplomacy and money, but with sword, if necessary. Rob insisted that Atticus join them, but in protective Tory green rather than a redcoat. Fitting him proved to be a challenge, but eventually he was sufficiently covered and adequately cryptic to protect against rebel sharpshooters. They set out at once, working westward from the army flank into the rich bottomlands on the banks of the Hudson. There was no resistance and farm after farm was shuttered and still, their barns empty of beasts and fodder. Even the few sympathetic folks who remained were barely existing on farmsteads decimated by Schuyler's men. At the end of the day, they returned to camp with less than a hundred weight of fodder gleaned from a score of emptied storerooms. Even more daunting was the lack of Tory soldiers for Burgoyne's army. Caleb had hoped that he might recruit additional men, but the rebels had warned them off, promising bad things would happen to those who supported their enemy.

29

With the Hudson now bridged, Burgoyne crossed over and continued south, carrying as much ammunition and supply as possible. A rebel group overwhelmed the small rear guard protecting the bridge, then destroyed it. The Royal Army was effectively isolated west of the Hudson with no direct road back to Fort Miller and Skenesboro. Days were growing cooler, prompting the army to burn watch fires long into the night, as much for warmth as for vigilance.

Rob saw Justice darting in and out of Burgoyne's headquarters frequently now and wondered what kind of intelligence the commander was getting. He shared his concern and knowledge of the man's scurrilous reputation in Boston with Caleb. But Caleb scoffed at the suggestion of Justice being a double agent. "Burgoyne knows that the man is a liar and is no longer taken very seriously by the war council. His estimate of thousands of rebel troops gathering to defend Albany is pure poppycock."

"Just be careful of that scoundrel," warned Rob, "He'll change his stripes in the blink of an eye!"

Burgoyne continued to push southward. Gates may have dithered, but did have the sense to order Colonel Morgan's Virginia sharpshooters to track British progress. By the middle of September, the Royal army had reached a place called Stillwater where he divided his column into threes and advanced on the colonials who, ever wary, disengaged regularly. Caleb's small contingent of Tories was assigned to Riedesel's Brunswickers proceeding along the road by the river. Their main task was to establish liaison with the main British columns advancing through the rougher, wooded country on their right. A sudden burst of unseasonable, muggy weather enveloped all combatants and grew hotter as the day progressed. The Germans became uncomfortable in their thick uniforms and cumbersome miters while hordes of bloodthirsty mosquitos harried their march. It seemed that the insects were aware that they had precious few days left for feeding before dropping temperatures would shut them down for another year. The redcoats advancing through the brushy and partially cleared woods suffered another marauder. Ticks. Deer had bedded there and dropped scores of tiny bloodsuckers that now clung to every bush, seeking attachment to anything with fresh, warm blood. Sergeants insisted that nothing was to disturb the prim lines and marching formation of their men and castigated soldiers attempting to sweep them off their uniforms. Before long, ticks would be the least of their worries.

Near noon the Brunswickers could hear sporadic popping of muskets in the forest. Judging it to be a mere skirmish, officers ordered the march to continue, but sent Caleb and his Tories into the forest to investigate. As Rob and Caleb crested a small knoll, they found the redcoats halted and clustering around several prone figures. "Officers!" Caleb muttered. "Damn rebel sharpshooters are picking off the officers." No sooner said than a musket ball whizzed by, clipping a hemlock branch above his head. Caleb ducked behind a fallen log, ordering his men to find who fired. "He can't be much more than 100 yards over there." He pointed with an outstretched arm just as another slug clunked into the punky deadfall.

In search parties of two the Tories melted into the forest. After an eerie silence, two muskets discharged in the underbrush. The Tories reappeared dragging a wild-eyed, wounded rebel dressed in buckskin, pleading for mercy with a southern drawl. "A Virginian," Caleb spat out derisively as a Tory sergeant coolly fixed his bayonet. The captive became frantic. "No, no, just shoot me!" He was well aware of the habit of Tory troops to skewer rebels. "No chance of that, man, but tell me to whose unit you render loyalty." The man looked at Caleb and the bayonet, but shook his head. Caleb nodded to the sergeant who responded with present arms, bayonet flashing in the sun.

The rebel yelped, then gasped. "I be one of Morgan's men. We been told to find the lobersterbacks for General Gates."

"And shoot English officers in the back whenever you can", Caleb added with a sneer.

Suddenly from the clearing in front of the stalled redcoats, a fusillade of musketry ended their conversation. Rob could see the rebels forming a line of battle. The British were also forming up despite possible harassment from Morgan's abominable marksmen. Caleb told Rob to see to the wounded man and called his small force together. The rebel's condition was not serious and the wound had stopped bleeding . Disarmed, he would be left on his own with Rob's full flask of water. Then the Tories retraced their steps to Riedesel and the Brunswickers on the river road. Riedesel sent a courier to Burgoyne asking permission to flank the Americans, receiving the terse reply, "Permission immediately granted".

As their lines formed the Royals found that resistance was stiffer than anticipated as a solid wall of musket fire poured into the redcoats. For a time, it seemed the British line would be penetrated and in real danger of collapse, but as the afternoon wore on, the German column near the river cut into the fight.

The rebels could not match the sudden firepower on their right flank and gradually retreated, leaving a bloodied and shaken enemy. Quite stunned, Burgoyne, on advice from his war council, gave the order to dig in and build several redoubts. Now the wait began. Rumors had it that Clinton was coming up the Hudson after all and information from Justice that the rebel numbers were nearly twice that of the Royal force urged Burgoyne to greater caution. Yet another issue was clouding his thinking. Diarrhea sickness was coursing through his troops. A soldier with his pants down would have great trouble aiming his Brown Bess.

Royal army fortunes grew more troublesome each day. Support from the rear had trickled down to near nothing and countryside scavenging was totally unproductive. With supplies and nourishment for his troops nearly depleted, Burgoyne gambled on another thrust the first week in October. This time he would drive even further into the forest and attempt to flank the colonials on their own turf. In charge of the foray was General Simon Fraser who had chased the rebels at Hubbardton. The advance had barely begun when it was met by three columns of rebels attacking all along the British line. The British wavered, then held and a seesaw conflict began. Fraser found he was losing officers to sharpshooters with ominous regularity. Germans were called in to hold the center of the line as Fraser boldly rallied his troops without concern for his own safety.

Daniel Morgan's sharpshooter peered down the long barrel of the Brown Bess that he had taken not a month before from a dead Hessian at Bennington. The .75 caliber weapon was heavy and nearly as tall as the slight Virginian who was puffing with effort and sweating profusely in the autumn heat.

As the scarlet line of fixed bayonets formed up in the clearing, he ignored them and ranged the sight on a distant red-coated rider. Calm and determined, ignoring the shock and panic among his buckskin-clad brothers, the soldier squeezed the trigger. The blast and smoke momentarily stunned him, but not before he saw the rider bend and hang loosely on the neck of his mount, before slipping to the ground. His horse, out of habit, continued to follow the blades of steel now pushing up a small hill.

So ended the career of Brigadier General Simon Fraser, the best of Gentleman Johnny Burgoyne's officers and perhaps the only one who could have rescued the British from the Saratoga debacle. His aide-de-camp rushed to the fallen general and quickly commandeered a wagon to transport his superior to a nearby farmhouse where Fraser expired despite efforts by Burgoyne's personal physician and Riedesel's wife.

Back in General Gates' headquarters, Arnold, sidelined by disagreements with Gates, emerged from a raucous quarrel with the commander. Unable to stay idle any longer, he mounted his horse and charged to the sound of musketry, urging the colonials to crash the Brunswickers behind their redoubt. But the Germans were too strong and held. Under fire, he galloped to a second redoubt where other Brunswickers, Caleb and his Tories hunkered.

Rob was in shock at the ferocity of the colonial attack and felt nauseous bile rising in his stomach. Suddenly, he involuntarily vomited at the sight of so many dead and maimed soldiers. The violence, confusion and stench of hot battle left him in a stupor. Terrified Germans bellowed in a tongue he could not understand save the cries of the wounded – "Mutter, mutter!" Only too well, he knew what that meant. Musket balls were pouring over the breastwork while both Hessian and rebel cannon roared, their lead missiles seeking soft targets. The musket fire was not really accurate beyond 100 yards, but the nearly three-quarter inch ball packed a wallop and a cannon ball the size of a fist could easily dismember a man. To his left a Hessian lay still, his shattered head lying some dozen feet away. Rob's face was splattered in a warm, gelatinous substance, the remains of the young soldier's brains. Father Henri's vivid descriptions of the fires of Hell paled in comparison to what he was witnessing. Head reeling, he peered over the breastwork to see a horseman driving hard upon his shelter. Caleb, too, was stunned when the horse and rider leaped among the Tories, slashing with his sword. His brain finally kicking in, Rob recognized Arnold yelling at troops "Boys, this way. Attack, attack!" Caleb rose up and saw the sword coming down just as he was shoved aside by a huge person in green uniform. Atticus. Arnold's blade cut deeply into Caleb's arm, but its energy was dissipated. Rob hugged the ground in terror.

The German defenders were now broken apart and in flight to the rear, but the Tories continued the fight. As Arnold wheeled his horse, a stray musket ball slammed into his left leg, the same one that had been maimed at Quebec City. His horse also took a ball and staggered, then fell with Arnold's leg pinned beneath the thrashing animal. Rob raised his head slightly and saw Arnold struggling to free himself. Crawling to the animal and enlisting the help of Atticus, they pushed and shoved with their feet. Suddenly, the mass of horseflesh moved away and Arnold rolled free, grasping his leg in pain. Their eyes met for an instant of recognition, then Arnold groaned his appreciation, but Rob was already scuttling to the breastwork where Caleb lay, his wound spurting bright blood. A lull in the fight had occurred when Arnold went down and the rebels hesitated just short of the breastwork, waiting for their reserves to come up, knowing that a few Tory muskets were still active. Rob pressed a piece of torn shirt over Caleb's wound and had him hold it fast to slow the bleeding.

Night fell, effectively ending the fight, but the Tories knew that the redoubt was indefensible. Come morning the rebels would be all over their position. In the dark, among the pitiful cries of rebel, redcoat and Hessian wounded, Rob and Atticus carried the semi-conscious Caleb back to the Great Redoubt, the last British stronghold. Recovery teams prowled the area searching for wounded. Rob flinched each time a gunshot cut the dark, knowing that some of the worst wounded were being put out of the way.

Arnold was found and carried back to a rebel hospital where he was treated immediately to prevent infection. For a time he thought he would lose the leg, but thanks to a durable constitution, he managed to settle for a slightly shorter appendage and locomotion with the help of a cane. Still, he chafed at the idea that his role as an active field commander was probably over. While the rank and file knew that it had been Arnold, the leader who inspired them to break the Royal army's back, Gates, in a jealous pique, saw to it that the brash general was hardly mentioned in the dispatches.

*   *   *

Justice ran his fingers over the stash of gold coins in his strongbox. With good reason he had never let anyone into his wagon and kept the locked box under the driver's seat out of sight. He always slept with the box next to his head and Lady Charlotte's wheel-lock pistol within reach. When he had to be away for a time, his trusted camp follower, Lucy, kept a close eye on his property. Lucy had been with him since before the strife in Boston and managed to know everything going on in the camp. Her unending flow of intelligence gathered from the women and their men had been invaluable to the rebels with whom he always had careful, if infrequent, contact. He smiled, knowing that the rebels always paid in hard currency for information about the pulse of the Royal army. That Burgoyne and his staff were also counting on him for reciprocal information on the rebels made things even better. He'd go back to Boston as a rich man.

But he was nobody's fool. Sooner or later this game would be up. One of these armies was sure to be defeated and before that happened he had to disappear. He stroked his neck and swallowed nervously at the thought of the rough strands of rope.

There was only Lucy. What to tell her and when? She would plead to go with him, but that was out of the question. Her young daughter, whom she adored, would be nothing but dangerous baggage when, in his usual fashion, he melted into Albany's social fabric.

30

The British army continued its retreat back to Saratoga. Surrounded by a huge American presence, Burgoyne surrendered his emaciated force to Gates, the Hero of Saratoga, on October 17, 1777. Understandably, Burgoyne's mood was dark as he agreed to the Convention of Saratoga in which his army was given parole under rebel control on the promise never to again make war on the colonies. But his depleted army was permitted to march out of camp with war honors and, by tradition, stack their weapons. The surrender, while a phenomenal boost to the fortunes of the victorious rebels, created an immediate dilemma. What to do with upwards of 6000 men plus women and children who were now dependent on the colonials. They would march to Boston for either confinement or deportation to England using some of the same route used by Knox and his cannons in 1775. Prisoners wishing to remain in America were allowed to escape, responsible for their own welfare. And many did, including a number of Brunswickers who gravitated to the German settlements in the Hudson Valley. In a shameful move in 1778, the colonial Congress, alleging a lack of cooperation from Burgoyne, suspended the Convention and kept the remaining prisoners in custody, moving them about the colonies, often under deplorable conditions, until the end of the war.

Rob and Atticus deposited their arms alongside those of the Royal army and waited to learn of their fate. Under Convention rules, the relatively small numbers of Tories, Canadians and Mohawks were free to go. This did not sit well with colonial rank and file, but, legally, they were considered the same as the potential escapees.

Caleb's saber wound had closed in response to skill by the Royal army physicians, but continued to swell and ulcerate. Several days before the surrender he was back in hospital with fever and delirium. This time he was bled and confined to bed. Though extremely weak, he desired to return to Skenesboro in Rob's care. Atticus would join them, as he had no wish to return to his master in Albany, having no proof of his release from bondage. And being on the losing side was hardly an asset. He would take his chances and begin a new life in Canada. Grateful for his saving his life, Caleb agreed to buy Atticus out of bondage. With what he was unsure, as his lands may have been confiscated making his net worth close to zero.

After exchanging their Tory green uniforms for farmer's homespun, they moved carefully north, half-carrying Caleb when his energy flagged. They avoided the forts and settlements, knowing full well that the rebels were mad as hornets and unforgiving of the role the Tories had played. Under cover of darkness, in a cold rain, they finally entered Skenesboro. Caleb, feverish and emaciated was immediately put to bed in his mansion where Phoebe and the servants took over his care. Rob and Atticus remained to assure that no one attempted to evict him or the Blairs.

For days, Caleb lay abed, weak and unresponsive to Phoebe's care. Then suddenly, he improved and surprised everyone by appearing in his study, pale, but steady. Within a week, he felt strong enough to travel and arranged to go north with the Blairs to Fort Ti that still remained in British control. Colonial militia had taken over most of the Elkinton and Skene estates and had picked clean their stables. He knew it was just a matter of time before he and his guests would be evicted. Adding misery, snow squalls had been moving down the lakes and would soon be buffeting Skenesboro.

Phoebe and Rob met in the garden amid piles of red and yellow leaves kicked up by a breeze off the lake. They embraced in the bower, but Rob knew that more than weather changes were in the air. Phoebe lost no time in telling him that she must go north with Caleb and her parents.

"My mother still needs much care and Caleb . . . well, Caleb also needs me."

"Do you love the man?" Rob wanted a direct answer.

Phoebe snuggled closer, momentarily raising Rob's hopes. But her silence was enough to give him the message. They remained close as Rob pressed her hands to his face. They were soft and nimble as the newly hatched birds he had handled as a boy. They recalled time years before while hunting when he had captured a newly fledged grouse chick. The hen had run up the trail ahead of him, wing distended in the usual decoy mode, while her nearly invisible offspring scattered in the underbrush. But Rob's sharp eyes had spied a stationary chick among the brown leaves and he had carefully picked it up, cupping his hands around the tiny puff of feathers as he now cupped Phoebe's hands. Now, as then, he felt the bright stirrings of soft life struggling to become free. He had released the chick gently and watched it scamper under the shrubs, soon disappearing as it became blended with the leaves. Could he do the same now? The pain of such loss wracked his being as he pressed her hands to his lips.

"How I will miss these, my bonnie bird." He slowly released them, letting his hands fall to his sides.

Their eyes met one last time and she smiled as she had in the bower so many times before. A gentle hand touched his lips, and then she turned and left the garden without another word. Rob continued to sit in the bower and felt the first few flakes of snow, becoming thicker with time like a final curtain forever separating him from Phoebe.

Caleb, Atticus and the Blairs left with their servants that very night, bundled against the cold and with only a few personal articles and possessions. Unbeknownst to the others, Caleb slipped a small pouch of money into Rob's hand, insisting that it was a vast underpayment for his services. He would not hear any refusal as Rob helped them launch the canoes into the chilly lake waters. Within minutes the canoes slipped quietly away to be swallowed by the snowy darkness.

31

Rob was in no hurry as he plodded up the Castleton road. Upon returning to the Elkinton mansion, he had secured it as best he could against the predations that were bound to come soon. Then, fully aware that he had no other place to go, departed for Hubbardton and the Acadian settlement. The snow squalls blowing in from the Adirondacks had passed quickly and the night sky was now clear. Starlight alone guided his feet over the rutted surface. Guerilla bands had been active here, harrying the few remaining British outposts, but he had no fear. The small pistol Caleb had insisted he take would protect him. But his conviction was that he would never use it. He had seen quite enough of carnage, the maimed bodies and the obscene din of battle. Those awful pleas for mercy or a quick death still rattled through his brain.

He turned and continued on the old military road, a lesser-used track now, which led to Hubbardton. Looking up at the uncountable stars burning down, he recalled Josh's claim that they had been there for thousands of years. But how could he know? All he learned was from those books kept under his bed — other men's musings. These lights would remain long after the armies had passed. Long after his own life was gone and forgotten, they would sparkle on whoever came along. Some would be called heroes, others fools and knaves, but all would live and die as part of a scurrying herd, who would, like him, be unimportant. Yet all of them, Knox, Francis and Fraser, Burgoyne and Arnold. Caleb and Atticus. The Abenaki, No Hair, Josh and Amalia. Ian and Tomsoc. Phoebe and Jenny. Yes, even poor Jenny. Rebels, Royals and Hessians. None of them could claim much or be long remembered under these stars. The all-enveloping dark seemed to press down, a crushing heavenly weight pressing the air from his lungs, like deep lake waters after a dive. Each star was a fire with no warmth, bright, but inaccessible. Everything he had done seemed insufficient, irrelevant, lost and broken beyond repair. Realizing suddenly that he was dog-tired, he stopped and lay on a bed of moss despite the cold. A few katydids out in the pitch-black forest continued their futile songs, barely scratching sounds from frigid wings. They, too, would be gone in a blink of an eye.

As he approached the cusp of troubled sleep, other names and faces swirled through his fevered brain. Singing Hessians. Tories in green. The Reverend Blair on his knees praying. Amalie, sweet Amalie. Rebel sharpshooters. His father, Ian, telling the settlement that taking sides would be their ruin. No Hair and the women mending broken bodies. The rouges, Justice and the Bartons.

"No one wins trying to destroy the other", he mumbled, losing consciousness.

*   *   *

The sky was brightening in the east as he shivered himself awake. He found a few wafers in his pack that did little to assuage the moans in his stomach. Slowly, a cold anger seeped into his gut on the thought of that peddler of vulgarity, Justice, who had been at the bottom so much trouble. He had not been seen since before the surrender. Chances were that he had gone over to the rebels, probably taking his mobile brothel with him. The whores would buy him status among the traders in Albany. Hoisting his pack, Rob's better judgement told him to perish any thoughts of the scoundrel. But, rounding a bend of the road, he came upon the blockhouse, its massive significance and menace, a sharp reminder of death and the tempest of destruction in this wilderness. For Jenny, Father Henri, for Amalie, for Tomsoc, he must know the truth. Bile rose in his throat and he knew that conflict was not over for him. Without hesitation, he turned and started back towards Skenesboro.

He avoided the main thoroughfare through Skenesboro and by dark was nearly to Fort Anne. He sought a meal at an isolated farmstead whose inhabitants were grateful for the hard currency he offered. An unusual spell of warm weather slid in and hovered over the Hudson while Rob moved on. His luck held as he found an uninhabited cowshed in which to comfortably spend the night. Farms were often abandoned as the conflict crawled its way towards Saratoga. Scavenging parties had carried off the livestock and Tory sympathizers had little courage to return to the area of hostile neighbors. Having successfully avoided restless bands of rebels, he entered the former Royal encampment two days later. Most of the captives had departed for Boston, but several camp followers remained, not sure of their future, but now serving rebel clientele. He easily infiltrated the militia holding the surrender site as just another soldier looking for lusty entertainment. Several ladies said they were available and took him off to their wagon. But once there he disappointed them by only asking questions about where the big teamster had gone. They made faces and cursed, but when he presented them the usual fee, they were most cooperative. Justice had left by wagon for Albany two days before with his favorite Lucy and her daughter.

"No reason he couldn't have taken us along, but the old bastard was too cheap. He always got his money and gave us leavings. Never worked a day in his life. Hope he ends up in the poorhouse."

Despite their elaborate enticements, Rob bade farewell to the ladies. He couldn't contain a grin as they made their faces again and called him a "light-stepper." But he wasted no time mixing with farmers and traders on the road to Albany, now seeing increased travel since the danger of invasion was over. It proved easy to hitch a ride on a trader's wagon, giving relief to his sore feet. He was soon in the commercial area near the docks where he knew that Justice would eventually set up his business given the frequent comings and goings of businessmen and watermen plying the Hudson. But it would not be easy to find the rouge's wagon in this busy hub. After two days search he was frustrated and getting low on money. He hired himself out to a merchant hauling grain via bateaux to New York City. The merchant recognized a strong back and carrying sacks of meal over a gangplank was but a small effort. He even found him a sheltered spot for sleeping in an adjacent grain warehouse. After a week, Rob began to think that Justice was elsewhere, perhaps pushing onward, bypassing Albany.

Late one afternoon as he left the boats he saw a weathered wagon parked near the warehouse. Normally, it would arouse no interest, but Rob spotted a worn Royal regiment symbol etched on the tailgate. Slipping into the door shadow of the warehouse, he avowed to keep an eye on the wagon. Darkness fell with no one claiming the vehicle, but out of nowhere emerged a skinny youth who climbed aboard and disappeared. Soon the person emerged lugging a small ledger. Moving quickly, the youth was nearly swallowed up among the crowd. Rob had difficulty trailing the youngster who finally turned to enter a slightly dilapidated boarding house several streets away from the waterfront. A number of transients were also entering, seeking an evening meal. Rob joined them and selected a seat on the darkened end of the long serving room.

"What'll it be, lad?" A plump serving wench was giving him a flirtatious eye. He had little appetite and was startled by her directness. But, recovering quickly, he ordered eels and bread.

"No grog for you?"

He brushed off the question and leaned back into the smoky darkness, wondering why he had come to this noisy, vulgar place. The youth was nowhere to be seen and the smoke was making his eyes water. The eels came and he decided to try the wench for information on a big teamster.

"Oh, you be looking for that, huh?" It was time to play along. "You stay here or come back later and there be a few women to buy." She tipped her cap slightly and smiled broadly, indicating that she might be one of them. He smiled back and asked who he would pay for these services. "Oh, there be a woman who is upstairs. She or her daughter will see to the business. The big driver with yellow teeth, he don't stir much, but we all knows who gets the money."

This was more than Rob expected to learn so quickly, now sure that Justice was upstairs. He finished his eels and plotted how to confront the culprit. It seemed the best way was to play along some more.

When the wench came near, he caught her eye and placed several farthings on the trencher.

"Show me the woman who makes the business."

The wench winked, picked up the trencher and glided away into the smoke. Suddenly, seeming to appear from nowhere, a young girl of perhaps a little more than a dozen years stood before him. She was slender and dressed as a boy. He was sure she was the same one who had been to the wagon. Despite the confounding garb, Rob saw a face on the cusp of becoming a desirable woman.

"What you want, sir?" The voice exiting from trembling lips was weak and without emotion. He noted that the eyes were large, even fearful, and hard as glass.

"Lucy, your mother, I need to see her." She gasped slightly, seemingly struck by this stranger's knowledge of her mother. "I mean no harm, child." he added. The stony eyes wavered, then looked at the several coins Rob had placed on the rough table. "Come with me." she whispered.

He followed her outside to a stairway leading to the second floor which opened to a hall with small rooms leading left and right. Incoherent, boozy male voices and giggles came from some of them, but the child continued to the end of the hall where she pointed to a door. Inside other voices were raised, one of them a growl Rob had heard before. He knocked and the argument ceased. The door cracked open and a woman with tears in her eyes asked what he wanted. Out of sight, the familiar voice bellowed. "You got another one, Lucy." She threw the door open as the girl dashed in front of Rob and hugged her mother. The room was spacious, nearly the size of the tavern below. A door at the end led somewhere probably to a trysting place like those they had seen in the hall. Justice froze when he saw Rob.

"What in hell do you want?" he scowled, then brightened. "Looks like the farm boy wants a little fun for the night. Come all the way to Albany for it. Now that's real funny with all them Frenchies laying around up country. Lucy, you and the young'un get to the other room while the lad here and me makes a deal." He looked greedily at the pouch Rob had hung around his neck.

"No deal." Rob announced, giving him a cold eye. "Just want to get something straight about what happened up at that blockhouse in the wilderness. A woman about to be married to my commander was shot and scalped and my Indian friend nearly hung for the murder he didn't do. You were the one telling the British that Indians did it, but that is untrue. The woman's guide escaped and told General Burgoyne that my friend had nothing to do with it. Yet you tried to make him hang for it. I want the truth."

Justice glared at Rob and took a step forward. The pistol tucked into Rob's trousers appeared in his hand. Justice breathed heavily and stopped. Then the wicked teeth showed as Justice began to see a way to get rid of this young thorn in his side.

"Tell you what. That time in the forest was long ago now and the Royal army be gone. Your friend didn't hang and your commander is probably chasing his ass into Canada. You and your shit-kicking Frenchies don't know nothing about how us teamsters live. I be a businessman who never killed anyone and I didn't kill that woman. Musta been one of my teamsters covering when she pulled a wheel lock on me. As for that drunk Mohawk, he shoulda known better. Can't ever trust those savages anyway."

He hesitated, then moved across to a dresser upon which sat a wooden box. Opening it, he palmed several gold coins. "Here, take this for the trouble I caused." Rob refused and firmed his grip on the pistol.

"Why should I believe you?" The turmoil in Rob's mind told him that Justice probably was truthful in saying he did not kill Jenny. To himself he pondered, "No, his evil kind never strike the blow, they just engage others to do that while basking in the delight of assault. Hadn't he done the same in Boston with the Bartons, in setting up Tomsoc for the gallows and who would know how many other nefarious deeds?"

Justice grinned. "Don't make much difference. Nobody is going to want to listen to some tale about a Tory accusing me of an accident while I was trying to help the rebel cause. Now put that there thing in your hand away and clear out of here before I loses my temper." Rob wavered and slid the pistol into his belt, but remained staring defiantly at the giant.

Justice laughed out loud. "Since yer here why not try out some of the girls. Better yet, you can have that one who brought you here." Rob took a deep breath at this suggestion, knowing full well now that he was looking at, as Father Henri would say, "the devil incarnate." Justice was the true heart of darkness.

"What's a matter, boy? Your first time? No worry. I had her myself this afternoon so she knows what to do." Rob now understood the stony look of terror in the young girl's eyes. The whoremonger's confession of violating this child made Rob's skin crawl. Here was depravity at its rawest. Rob cringed, recalling the terror in the young girl's eyes.

Neither Rob nor the giant noticed that the door at the end of the room had remained open. Coming across the threshold was Lucy, face screwed in pain and Lady Charlotte's wheel lock in her hand. "You bastard," she hissed at Justice. "You've taken everything you could from me and the other women and now you've taken my daughter. Ruined her! Even offering her up to this bumpkin!" Her voice rose to shrill, a trollop scorned in the extreme.

For the first time, Justice showed alarm, but not to lose control, began to pander. "Oh, Lucy, it want like that at all. The girl asked it. Like you, she wants to be like the other women." He turned and dug into his box. "Here, take this and buy her some new clothes", he mumbled, searching deeper into the box. Suddenly he bellowed. "Where's the rest of the money? I told that girl to bring up everything in my chest from the wagon." Lucy smiled slightly for the first time. "All she got was the ledger you asked for. The gold is still down on the street."

During this domestic exchange, Rob had been forgotten. When Justice glared at Lucy and took a step toward her, he raised his pistol again, but not before the wheel lock went off. Justice paused, eyes full of surprise, then gripped his gut. The heavy caliber ball, normally enough to knock a man down only swayed Justice. "What you do that for, Lucy?" he murmured, almost sweetly. Then, stumbling forward, he brushed her aside and lurched out the door, making for the stairs. "Got to get my gold." he cried and kept going.

Rob was in shock. Lucy collapsed on the floor in the arms of her daughter, the wheel lock sliding away on the carpet. With a mournful wail, Lucy tried to get up. "Justice, you got to come back. I done what I had to. She's better than us and what we had all these years."

Rob retrieved the wheel lock and helped the girl move Lucy to a chair. "Let him go." Rob said forcefully. "He'll never make it to his wagon." And Rob was right. Justice hobbled down the side street, then fell in the gutter within sight of his wagon, clawing with his hands on the cobbles trying to make more distance. Finally, the clawing stopped and he lay still, a deep red stain oozing over the stones. That's where the boarders would find him next morning. He was just another drunk who had been on the losing side of an argument with his cronies.

Rob told the two women to stay in their room. Chances were that Justice was dead and they could come out next morning for a bogus search. It was over for them now. With the din and commotion downstairs in the tavern, the shot would have gone unnoticed. No one need know what happened in the boarding house. Lucy and her child could take whatever gold Justice kept in his strongbox and go somewhere to make another life. He would keep the wheel lock so the investigating constable would never know what weapon was used in the killing. He left the boarding house by the front door smiling, never seeing the wench whose face registered a dejected frown. Outside, he slipped into the dark, making for the Hudson, for Skenesboro.

32

No Hair awoke with a start, heart pounding, stirred by her own groaning and mewing. The other women nearby turned in their beds uncomfortably. They had often heard No Hair's cries in the night as she relived the trauma. There was little they could do, but one now arose and went to comfort her. Breathing heavily, No Hair swooned in the encircling arms, head shaking wildly. "Tomsoc, must see Tomsoc," she cried and dashed out into the dark. Since Josh had left, Tomsoc slept in a shed near the barn to be protector of the animals. When very cold weather arrived he would move into an upstairs garret at the inn. No Hair pounded on the shed door until he flung it open expecting to see a marauding animal. She nearly fell across the threshold into Tomsoc's arms.

"Go easy, mother. Now sit here on the step and tell me of the demons you suffer." He had calmed her many times before, listening to the mumbled fears and mewings.

"Rob. Must find Rob." Her head began to shake followed by her whole body. "Come, quickly with me to Skenesboro to find him."

Tomsoc hesitated, but only briefly, knowing that No Hair's visions, while strange, were often prophetic of danger or trouble. He gathered two robes, flinging one over No Hair's shoulders and they stole away into the dark.

Rob was certain that both Tories and Rebels returning to their homes would now have need for his labor to rebuild ravaged farms. He would work his way to Skenesboro and beyond, eventually to Canada, find Phoebe and settle with her on land somewhere near the St. Lawrence. It would be difficult in the near term, but they would soon prosper. His confidence and gait quickened each day. Arriving in Skenesboro, he hired himself out to the same lumber mill that had provided Arnold with his navy. Only a light snow lay in the woods, but by working expertly with the oxen, Rob snaked out logs better than anyone else. Some days later, as night fell, he whistled merrily upon returning to the mill with a final bundle of logs, knowing that after only two weeks of effort he had sufficient resources to carry him to Canada.

Lost in grandiose plans and euphoria, he nearly stumbled over Tomsoc who emerged noiselessly from a dense clump of hemlock. Startled, he halted the team and peered carefully through the dusk at the Indian barring his way, his hand tightening on the primed wheel lock under his tunic. Tomsoc stood silently, waiting for recognition. Rob brightened and greeted his friend openly. "Tomsoc, you have found me, I know not how, but why are you here?"

The Abenaki merely stepped aside, allowing No Hair to emerge from the copse. Rob embraced her small form and repeated his question. She returned his greeting, but remained speechless, unsmiling, eyes riveted on Rob. His happiness suddenly waned and a knot of anxiety squirmed into his gut.

"What have you come to tell me?" His voice was thick and guarded. "Is my father dead? What of Amalie? What of Josh? The settlement?"

No Hair came right to the point. "No, nothing is wrong. It is you who are troubled. The sachem and Father Henri came to me in a dream and told me to find you. Why are you about to depart for Canada? You have forgotten about our life by the lake. A terrible worm has entered your insides. It has caused many pockmarks there, like this face you see before you. It will continue to grow and soon your heart will fall out just as did my hair," She snatched off her headpiece and revealed the smooth scalp. Few had seen this bare head save a few Acadian women with whom she washed and slept.

Rob turned away from those eyes, this sudden unmasking. To himself, he asked, "Why is she exposing herself this way? How did she know where I was going? How did these Abenakis find me out here in these woods?"

No Hair continued. "You seek a young woman with unblemished hands who has left for the north with a man of her choosing. Yet the worm makes you think she is still yours. He will drive you on until one day your heart falls out and he will laugh. You will wander further and further into the north and one day you will forget what you were seeking. Each day will fill your eyes with blowing dust and snow water instead of blood will flow through your channels. You will find a lake and it will beckon your snow water as its own which you will then gladly give and slide to your home beneath, becoming just food for the animal spirits waiting there."

"This old women is crazy with her tales of dreams and spirits," thought Rob. "Surely her Abenaki companion harbors no such illusions." He searched Tomsoc's face for support, but found only a set jaw.

"The two of you. You come here to tell me I live by wrong rules that I have decided to obey. Yet, they are my own, not those of others. You wish to remain simple and find strength in the rules of others. That is your choice. I have made mine." He flicked his switch over the heads of his oxen and prepared to continue to the mill.

Tomsoc now stood in front of him. "Our friend, Josh, has left the settlement for good to make his way in a world he knows better than ours. But he has no worm. He will take with him always what the settlement has given with him. Your father's heart has ached since you left and needs you to help him soon with next season's preparations." The Abenaki let some blowing snow drift between them.

"And Amalie cannot run the inn by herself, despite her energy."

Rob gazed at his friends and said nothing, but touched Tomsoc's shoulder in friendship, then flicked the switch over the oxen again and trudged on to the mill.

*　　*　　*

Tomsoc tried his hand at hunting turkey on the ridge that overlooked the lake. His keen sense of nature told him that as evening fell the birds would be flocking to roost in the robust, dense oak trees lying out of the wind wafting up from the watery swale. Their leaves still hung in dull browns, perfect cover to hide the large birds. Elsewhere, except for the scattered beeches, foliage had been stripped bare, the hardwoods were ready for whatever winter might bring. He waited for a clear shot on the wood's edge. A slight movement on the summit drew his eye. A man was standing behind a boulder, gazing out to the lake. Just his jacketed arm was visible, but Tomsoc knew that it wasn't one of the settlement. Soon the figure turned and looked directly at Tomsoc. The failing light and distance made it unlikely that Tomsoc could be seen against the dusky oaks. The Abenaki recognized Rob at once. Delighted, he considered hailing his friend, then thought better of it and turned away, heading for the settlement.

He sought out Amalie who was just finishing her chores at the cowshed. Tomsoc smiled and told her to go to the ridge. He would finish her work. Rob had returned. "He is here?" she gasped and eyes wide, she stepped lively, despite her burden, the two miles to the ridge.

Rob was seated where he and Amalie had once listened to the spring peepers. Amalie spotted him from afar and hesitated, biting her lip in anguish. Just go back and let him come to the settlement and find his father, his friends . . . . find her! She still had her pride. What if he was changed, as she had long feared? Perhaps he was but on his way to Fort Ti and Canada as No hair had predicted? Suddenly it was too late to turn tail. He had looked up and spotted her. She walked more slowly now while he continued to sit, his face inscrutable in the dim light. She hesitated and came no closer.

"Hello, Amalie. You are safe and well in the settlement, I presume.", he uttered indifferently, his posture a mixture of caution and regret. She nodded and stood her ground.

"We feared for you, Rob." But now to see you back is fine. It is what we all wished."

He looked away and remained mute. She felt herself giving way to her worst fears, but rallied quickly, knowing his penchant for hiding his feelings. She had learned his bent for reticence early on in their childhood. She didn't know why, but suspected it was a trait given him from his Scots father. Yet, his body language seemed to say that he was grateful for her presence.

"Will you go or will you stay, Rob?" She preferred the direct answer and stepped closer to better view his face. He turned and noticing her swelled belly, became rigid. Amalie seated herself on the rock and waited.

Finally, Rob muttered, "It's Josh's bairn, right?"

"Oh no, Rob" she laughed. "It's ours, yours and mine. Rob, you happily gave me this baby in the cowshed loft. Don't you remember?" Rob turned and considered the swale below, now silent and ice-filled.

"If you have come to stay . . . . with us . . . with me, I must know that your head will be as happy with me as your loins. Please tell me it will be that way for us. I wish not to love a ghost of what was."

He turned and gazed squarely into her face, ruddy now with the wind coming over the ridge.

"Yes, my dear Amalie, it is and will be so. I had not the sense to see that you and I have always been on a single road together." He clasped her hands and pressed them to his lips. "It will always be thus." he repeated, burying his face in her hair. The winter wind was slowly shifting to the north out of Canada, but they were little aware of its sharp chilling bite. There was nothing more said as they embraced.

EPILOGUE

Caleb and Phoebe, 1777-1807

The canoes bearing Atticus, Caleb, Phoebe and the Blairs made their way to Fort Ti where they were given protection and welcomed by Lady Charlotte and Lord Penfield. As Burgoyne's captive army marched across Massachusetts, the Fort Ti commander razed the bastion and retreated north with its few defenders to Canada. Atticus insisted that Jeremy, now recovered, join them and Caleb and his charges finally reached Quebec in late November.

The surviving colonial prisoners at Fort Ti were released prior to the fort's destruction and those needing additional medical attention made their way to the Acadian settlement. After healing, many returned to their farms in southern New England, but a few stayed on in appreciation of their care and recognition of the settlement's efficient agriculture.

After the peace accord in 1783, Caleb returned to Skenesboro and successfully petitioned payment for his house and lands. Caleb freed both Atticus and Jeremy after purchase from their former owners. The Reverend Blair married him and Phoebe in 1784 and they purchased land south of the St. Lawrence River. Caleb invested in shipping and became both successful and wealthy, leaving his lands and business to Phoebe and their three children upon his death in 1807.

BENEDICT ARNOLD, 1777-1801

It took nearly a year for Arnold to recover from his wounds. As was his nature, he brooded still over his failure to be given appropriate rank, the incompetence of the Continental Congress and its political intrigues. Not one to hide his light under a bushel, he quarreled with Congress itself and the other self-seeking generals. General Washington, who seemed to have a respect for this restless warrior, assigned him to command in Philadelphia while he practiced getting around with his shortened left leg. That assignment may have led to his final despicable decision to trade sides and become a soldier for the crown. Philadelphia, the capital of the rebel Congress, was a hotbed of intrigue, full of accusations and investigations, many of them spurious. His old enemies tried to diminish his reputation by accusing him of using his position for illicit business deals. A court-martial cleared him of all but a few petty charges. He was mildly admonished by Washington, but the damage was done. A series of setbacks for the rebel armies, including soldier mutinies, may have exacerbated Arnold's dark mood.

In Philadelphia, a pretty young Tory who soon became his wife had entranced him and at sometime, perhaps with her encouragement, the inward brooding got the best of him. Washington gave him the chance to get out of the capital and he opted for the command of West Point, the main defensive structure on the Hudson. Thinking that the British army might give him the glory he sought, he made contact with a Major John Andre who had been one of his wife's earlier acquaintances. Andre was an adjutant general in the British army and the two contrived to turn the details for the defense of West Point over to the British.

But Andre was captured with the plans bearing Arnold's name. Arnold himself barely escaped to a British sloop anchored in the Hudson not far from West Point. He arrived in New York where he was made a Brigadier General and awarded a hefty prize of British sterling. Andre was less lucky and received a spy's reward of death on rebel gallows.

Arnold's reputation as a British brigadier was less spectacular than his role with the rebels. He led raids in Virginia and Connecticut that had little to do with the war's outcome. His leadership in the Groton Connecticut raid assured him the enmity of his fellow neighbors when the attack went amuck and his subordinates massacred both opposing soldiers and captives. His actual involvement in this sorry affair has never been proven, but the shame lingered. Returning to New York, he soon became disenchanted with the British commander, Sir Henry Clinton, who dithered instead of going after Washington's fragile army. After Yorktown, he must have felt like a rather big fish out of the water. He and his wife departed to London in 1782, never again to visit his country. He was granted a pension from the British government and soon entered the mercantile business with his sons in New Brunswick, Canada.

His business dealings brought him to Quebec on occasion and there he made contact with Caleb's company. Both of the old combatants were astonished when Arnold limped into Elkinton's office, located in the lower town. Arnold was on his best behavior as he shook hands and sipped a bit of the sherry offered. Arnold's reputation was well known by this time and Caleb cordially declined the offer of a joint shipping proposal.

"Thanks, but no thanks, General Arnold." Caleb settled back in his chair and noted a trace of pain on Arnold's face. In a flash it was gone and Arnold continued. "Well, just thought I might try, Elkinton."

"Say, I'm glad you still have good use of that arm. Shouldn't have been so fired up to slice you at Saratoga. I'm sorry. Guess we're just two miserable war-horses now, me with this gimpy leg and you with that scar."

Caleb thought for a moment, then called out, "Atticus and Jeremy, come here." The two blacks emerged from the back room and stared at Arnold for a time. He stared back, a bit dumbfounded.

"This is General Arnold, Atticus, the one who jumped into our position at Freeman's Farm." Atticus scowled and said nothing.

Turning to his visitor, Caleb continued. "General Arnold, this man saved my life that day, then helped free you from your wounded horse. Do you recall?"

"Ah, yes, I do and many thanks to you sir and that Acadian lad who helped you."

Atticus finally smiled. "Maybe I shoulda left that nag on top of you, after all the grief you give us."

Arnold breathed out loudly and gazed out the window across the Saint Lawrence. "That's Levis over there where we spent a hellish winter neigh 20 years ago. Young Montgomery died not three streets from where we stand. The worst of luck. None of us would be here now if he and I had been successful."

"Well, that was long ago and here we all are. Please believe me when I say I'm much obliged for the sherry." He rose stiffly and bade them farewell, limping off down the street. Jeremy had said nothing to this point, but now shook his head and uttered, "Poor man, he still fighting his war." Caleb and his assistants watched Arnold in silence until he rounded a corner, then turned their attention to the affairs of the day.

Arnold eventually returned to England where he died in 1801. He'd become something of a pariah among his acquaintances and forever held treasonous by his former countrymen, an unfortunate epitaph for the best tactician and field general of the American Revolution.

Westenhook, 1782

Josh wiped sweat from his neck as he watched the last load of corn make its way up the dusty lane to the barns where his several Brunswickers would put it away in the storage cribs. The former Hessian soldiers were good workers even if language was still a problem. These two had deserted Burgoyne's army as it passed through the Berkshires on the way to Boston. Josh had left the settlement shortly before Rob's return, knowing that his time there was over and that his continued attraction to Amalie would rupture both his friendship with Rob and provoke disharmony in the settlement.

He would make new beginnings in the west. As farm manager, Josh had been able to convince his Dutch employers, the Van Duesans, that these men would be worthy hires and so successful were the Germans that they now called Westenhook, the most easterly reach of the Dutch patroon system, their home. With a huge estate of more than 800 fertile acres near the Housatonik River to care for, the Van Duesans needed all the dependable hires they could find and, conversely, treated all their employees with fairness and generosity.

Turning his mount toward the barn, he noted a horseman coming up the lane from the main thoroughfare, kicking up a cloud of dust. Visitors were rare at this busy harvest time. "What news is this?" he wondered. As the rider came closer, Josh recognized his old friend Tomsoc whom he hadn't seen since leaving the settlement.

After a joyful reunion, Tomsoc smiled broadly. "I have a document for you. It came to the settlement and Rob and Amalie insisted that I personally deliver it to you." Then he laughed out loud and added, "It was not hard to find you. The school from which I fled is just over that mountain in Stockbridge." He paused, looking up at the crags of Squaw Peak.

Josh opened the sweat-stained parcel, the victim of nearly a week in the saddlebag. Inside was a document prepared on fine, durable paper.

"To all interested persons:

Be it known that Joshua Shattuck, formerly indentured servant to The Brothers Barton, Ironmongers in Boston, Massachusetts, is hereby released from indentured status as the result of payment in full for his services and time to said brothers above by Mr. Henry Knox, Major General, Continental Army."

Payment received in full by:

_____X_____ his mark, J. Adams, Esq.
Ethan Barton

_____X_____ his mark, J. Adams, Esq.
Noah Barton

This is a true copy attested to by:

_____

John Adams, Esquire
Braintree, Massachusetts
May 15, 1782

Josh was struck dumb, his heart swelling in his breast and could say nothing.

Tomsoc smiled broadly. "I know how you feel. My kinsmen tell me that the school from which I escaped has been closed and the teacher clergyman has died. I need not fear returning to the few friends there who now remain.

Finally, Josh found his voice and muttered, "Then we are both free now, friend." As he clasped the Abenaki's hand firmly, he noted, taut and healthy, the raised, red scar on the arm, covering muscle that rippled strong and sure below. "You will stay? I need you here for the harvest."

Tomsoc nodded and they rode in silence to the house in the shadow of Squaw Peak where a supper and cool water awaited.

It was no surprise to his friends that Josh, in later years, was drawn to a group called the Shakers, a religion established by its matriarch, Mother Ann Lee. Shakers espoused ideals of the Quaker faith, but were strict proponents of simplicity and efficiency in work and personal habits. Josh never married and left the Van Duesan Westenhook estate to be with the fledgling Shaker community in Hancock, Massachusetts where he remained for the rest of his life

Hubbardton 1797

Save Amalie, no one was happier to welcome his prodigal son than Ian MacKensie. Although the settlement had suffered during the warfare along the lake, it had remained intact. The withdrawal of the British army may have eliminated open conflict, but as the war wound down, sporadic raids by Tory guerillas and British regulars kept the Acadian transplant on edge, to say nothing of continued influx of New England colonists always hungry for land. Increasing age and pain from the old wounds had slowed Ian down and he needed Rob's strength to hold the settlement together.

The newly declared Republic of Vermont did little to ease their burdens what with questionable British overtures to help the new government and jealous claims on Vermont territory by New Hampshire men and Yorkers alike. But after the peace accords in 1783 discord quieted down and the settlement farms, enjoying new freedoms in the Vermont Republic, continued and improved their efficient ways. The inn became a regular stop for travelers to and from the southern New England states and Canada. Rob and Amalie became highly recommended as host and hostess by guests.

When Ian passed on in 1790, he went with a smile on his disfigured face. He was laid next to his wife and the stillborn son. No Hair followed soon after and was placed by Father Henri, a colorful new cap on her head fashioned by the Acadian women and her hands clutching his crucifix. Years later, when war again threatened the lakes, Rob and Amalie held fast to neutrality and weathered the storm. Their sons, Ian and Caleb, saw that both sides in this conflict were well supplied with food and fodder, assuring that the settlement continued to prosper.

One fine summer day in 1797 a carriage drew up to the inn and two elderly passengers stepped out into the Vermont sun. Amalie emerged from the kitchen, a bit of flour clinging to her hands and welcomed them. She was stunned when the well-dressed lady embraced her, flour and all. It was Lady Charlotte who then introduced Lord Penfield. Josh came in through a back door and was speechless. Lady Charlotte laughed. "You'd think we were ghosts by the look on your faces. In our old age we thought it best to come thank you in person for the care you gave us those years ago."

"You are most welcome to our home and inn," Rob declared, grasping the Lord's hand. They retired to the porch which Rob and Tomsoc had put on the inn prior to Tomsoc's departure to Westenhook where he now lived with Josh. It overlooked the lake and a cool breeze wafted over the fields leading down to the water, not a quarter mile away. A young woman appeared carrying tumblers of cool spring water. She had features remarkably like those of Amalie, which were immediately and quietly noted by Lady Charlotte. Despite differences in speech and station, none had difficulty in sharing their lives over the past 20 years.

"You rebels have done well," enjoined Lord Penfield, whose use of the term got a sharp look from his Lady. "Don't worry about that, please," laughed Rob. "We never thought of ourselves as coming in on either side. It was hard to tell whether you, the Hessians or the Continentals and militia gave us the most trouble."

"But tell us, what became of General Burgoyne?"

"Oh, him." It was Lady Charlotte's turn to laugh. "He returned to England quite embarrassed and was dragged through the political turmoil for a while, but his interest soon returned to the theater . . . and the performers." She grasped her husband's hand and continued. "He took up with a singer and they had several children. Poor man, he had lost his wife just prior to heading the invasion army. He is now an old man who has regained most of his dignity, and spends many days enjoying theater and music as he always did."

While Amalie told of their rustic life in Hubbardton, Rob left for his study. Returning, he held a wheel lock pistol which he declared was unloaded. He passed it to Lady Charlotte, saying, "This is yours, I believe." She was stunned and stammered. "Why . . . . Where did you get it? I last gave it to Jenny before that awful murder" Her eyes filled with tears that she whisked away with a fine handkerchief.

"It was taken from her by those responsible for her death and was given to me by a teamster at a boarding house in Albany after the surrender." He declined to elaborate further and soon saw a look of understanding in Lady Charlotte's eyes.

"We have no use for it here, so please keep it."

She looked at Lord Penfield. "Yes," he responded, "and we will give it to our friend, General Burgoyne. He has precious few memories of any kind now and despite his military fall from grace like an old war-horse, he recalls his days in the Royal army with fondness. We, of course, shall not tell him the odyssey of the weapon."

The late afternoon light, drew their conversations to a close and they retired to a special dinner prepared by Rob and Amalie's daughter and the inn staff. The next morning, preparing to leave, Lady Charlotte drew Rob aside.

"Do you have any message for Caleb and Phoebe, Rob? We will see them before boarding ship in Quebec."

Rob smiled. "Please tell them that Amalie and I are most content and that we pray their health and fortunes are equal to ours." She waited, but knew that Rob would add nothing more.

On the porch, she found Amalie sweeping out the dust of the previous day. She grasped her hands and brought her close. "You and Rob are most fortunate, Amalie." She dropped her eyes. "Long ago I told you that our lives drifted in separate seas and I still believe that. But you seem now to have refreshing and bountiful freedom here that, as a woman, I still only dream about in England. We may enjoy very different people and places, but you and your kin have developed a bedrock of simplicity and clear-eyed liberty in your bones. Is that what life in this settlement has done?"

Amalie smiled, recalling the years of hard but satisfying life. "I never thought of it that way, but perhaps it is true."

Lady Charlotte continued. "The tempest has passed away, thank God, but it may be longer before most of us learn to share freedom with others and rid ourselves of social prejudice and disrespect."

She hesitated, then cautiously added, "Do you see contentment and happiness in Rob's eyes? Does he treasure you and all that you have?"

Amalie nodded. "Yes, every day." She then responded with a laugh and clasped Lady Charlotte's smooth, unblemished hands in her rough ones. "And our small sea lies there", she pointed out across the fields to the lake. "We've learned to love our simple life and know it is where we ought to be." As she pressed the titled woman in a farewell embrace, Amalie's eyes sparkled like the gentle swells of the lake waters.

ACKNOWLEDGMENTS

Holyoke Community College generously assisted with technical support in writing this novel.

My thanks also go to Patrick Delgado Lavallee who provided crucial digital advice and fixes for map images in the text.

I am most grateful to my wife, Peggins, for her patient help in navigating Microsoft Word and constructive comments on story structure.

Shortcomings in style and errors in presentation of this work of fiction are mine alone.

LaVergne, TN USA
15 August 2010
193409LV00003B/518/P

9 781450 059268